Paula sensed her danger, gave a long shuddering sigh and went absolutely limp in his arms. Sid released her abruptly. She staggered and caught her balance and moved back away from him.

"What do you think I am?" she asked in a rusty indignant whisper.

"That's what I'm trying to find out."

"Turn on the lights."

"Shut up," Sid said. He put his hand against her shoulder and shoved hard to send her sprawling across the bed, hissing with alarm. He went to the window and lifted one of the flaps of the venetian blind and looked across at cabin number thirty-four. He saw no one anywhere near it. A light went on behind him. He dropped the flap, put the night chain on the door and turned to look at her. Paula was standing by the bed, looking disheveled and smeared and indignant. Sid picked the purse up, hefted it thoughtfully and took it to her.

"There's the bathroom. Fix yourself up. Stay away from the phone and we can get along just fine . . ."

on the run

by John D. MacDonald

An Original Gold Medal Book

GOLD MEDAL BOOKS

Fawcett Publications, Inc., Greenwich, Conn.
Member of American Book Publishers Council, Inc.

one

IN HIS dreams there was light and color, remembered faces and old accusations, and in his dreams his voice seemed to go on and on, explaining, justifying himself to skeptics.

But he would come out of the dreams, out of a remembered litheness, back into a body ninety-two years old, to the hush of a house of illness. He knew his impatience was irrational. The body had always healed itself in time. Sickness had always been temporary. But this business of dying seemed to involve so much waiting.

He envied the other old ones, dying all over the world, envied them for their blurred minds which made brief and glancing contacts with reality. But he in turn could be envied, he knew. There was no pain. The lower spine was gone, the legs dead. And there was the money, of course. Money kept you from dying among charitable strangers. Money was a deodorant, keeping you sweet and sanitary and inoffensive despite the mess of helplessness. But how the clear mind roamed all dimensions of the mortal trap, deploring past acts, dreading blackness, whining about truth.

He looked at the angle of the mid-summer sun, then turned his head and looked at his gold watch in its small wire stand on the table beside the bed. Ten minutes after three, and a time of dreaming which had not been wasted because, for a little while, he had visited the summertime of 1884, bringing the little blue sloop back across Caydo Lake in a squall, the year it was new, his mother on the dock anxiously awaiting him, taking the line he threw her as the sail came rattling down. Dreams are the time machines, and this one would give him a

5

lot of new things to remember about his fourteenth summer.

He reached his right hand down to the frame of the bed and found the button which began the soft humming, the slow raising of the head of the bed. He was glad he had ordered them to move him into the small library off the living room of the old house. The master bedroom had been too traditional a room to die in. He had tried the living room next, but it was the house in which he had been born, and too many caskets populated his memories of that room, too many candles and waxy faces, too often the ripe sweet smell of the flowers. A sardonic amusement sufficed for a time to offset this awareness, but in May he had decided to be moved into the library, had them take the old desk out, place the bed where he could see, when sufficiently elevated, the red maples and a part of the neglected garden, and a segment of iron fence and stone wall.

Paula Lettinger came in, almost without sound. She went to the foot of the bed and looked at him with a mocking severity.

"You have a bell, you know," she said.

"Young woman, when I need your attentions, I shall be happy to summon you."

She came to him, touched his pulse, touched his forehead, shifted the pillows slightly. She was a dark-haired woman in her late twenties, with heavy black brows, a long firm body, high strong youthful breasts. Her skin had an ivory clarity, and her face had flat planes, prominent cheekbones under the eyes deeply set. He knew that the look of her was a remote heritage, remembering that her paternal grandmother had Onandaga Indian blood, had been a rebellious girl, a victim of gossip, had married the Lettinger who had failed in the livery stable business, had borne him three sons, had died of influenza in 1918, along with Lettinger and one of the boys.

She wore slacks and a sleeveless yellow blouse. He had insisted she give up the white garments of her trade, sensing that in so doing, she would also relinquish some of that professional impersonal bustling of the trained nurse.

He saw the new touch of color on her nose and cheeks, and across her forehead. "Was it pleasant in the sun?"

She was startled for a moment. "You're a sly old one. Yes it was. I sat at that old cement table and wrote letters. In shorts and a halter, if you need all the details. And the Ormand boy climbed a tree and stared over the fence at me."

"His taste is admirable and his manners are foul. Did you write to your husband?"

She had moved to the foot of the bed. "I wish you wouldn't call him my husband. The marriage was annulled."

"All right. The man who was once your husband."

She sighed. "I wrote to him. My God, how you bully me!"

"How do you feel about it, now that you've written?"

"A sense of relief, I guess. But I'd hate to admit you might be right."

"Everybody must be given a chance, and another, and another, as many as the heart can endure, Paula."

"Jud doesn't deserve another chance."

"Who are you to judge? Five years in prison can change a man. If he wants to see you when he gets out next week, he should have the right to know where you are, the right to come and explain or apologize—the right to know there is somebody in the world who has a little less than absolute hate for him. The thing I most bitterly regret in my life is my righteousness, my dear."

She sighed and shrugged. "If he comes here, I'll talk to him. It won't change anything. But I guess he should have that chance anyway. At least now you'll stop hounding me. Jane has made some divine chicken broth."

"Not right now."

"It will have to be right now. A man has come to see you. If you don't have the broth, he'll have to wait until tomorrow."

"Probably some pest."

"Oh, I know he's a pest. And he's cost you a great deal of money in the past year. Chasing wild geese."

"Fergasson!"

"The broth is delicious."

"But my dear girl, if he comes here rather than sending written reports, it means he has something impor . . ."

"A very delicate flavor."

"It is wicked and unprofessional for you to agitate a sick old man."

"As soon as you start on the broth, I'll phone him."

"It astounds me that you should call me a bully, Miss Lettinger. Bring the broth. Please do."

She came back to his bedside after phoning Fergasson at the Bolton Inn. Fergasson would be out at four o'clock. He sipped the broth slowly. It seemed to have no taste, only heat and wetness. He told Paula about the little blue sloop and the faraway summer.

"And I found a dog I had forgotten," he said. "Bismarck. His namesake was alive then, settling affairs with blood and iron. The dog looked savage. He had a basso bark, but blue jays used to chase him, and he'd hide under the stable."

"Back to the beginnings," she said in a gentle voice. She sat on the deep window seat, outlined against the sunshine. "That's what I was trying to do, coming back here."

"I thank God you did, my dear. I can hear them when you go into the village, all their sour little mouths flapping. See her? That's Paula Lettinger. Came back here and got a job nursing old Tom Brower, and him dying of every disease known to man and taking his sweet time about it, her shut up in that gloomy old pile of rock Tom's daddy built out of the money that came from overcharging the Union Army for uniforms. Just old Tom there and old Jane Weese been housekeeping for him for thirty years, and feeble old Davie Wintergreen, lives out in the back and does the yard work. Hear tell she's got a husband locked up in jail due out soon."

"Don't, Tom. Please don't."

"Paula, my dear, the vulgar and ignorant of this area have spent an appreciable percentage of their empty lives discussing the intimate affairs of the Brower family, and God knows we've given them enough material over the years. And this . . . final mission of mine, which certainly they have heard about and distorted to suit their temper, must be giving them a splendid finale."

They heard the door chime. She got up quickly and went through to the front hallway and let Adam Fergasson in. He was a slender and muted little man, with a smile of servility contradicted by such a flavor of self-importance that he seemed the image of the clerical public servant the world over.

But when young Randolph Ward, Tom Brower's attorney, had been directed to contact the best investigation firm in the country and ask them to assign their best man to Brower's mission, Adam Fergasson had appeared to be interviewed.

The mission could be simply stated, though the clues were vague: Find my two grandsons. Find them before I die.

Fergasson had nodded, made notes, asked only the most pertinent of questions, and had gone away.

Now he came into the library in his dark suit, murmuring his hope that Mr. Brower was having a good day, taking a straight chair at Brower's right, looking pointedly at Paula Lettinger.

"Miss Lettinger will stay with us, Mr. Fergasson," the old man said.

"Very well," Fergasson said. He took a dark notebook from an inside pocket. A little gleam of pride was evident as he said, "I have located Sidney Shanley. He is going by the name of Sid Wells. He is working as a used car salesman in Houston, Texas. He does not stay in one place very long."

"Are you absolutely certain?"

"I am positive, Mr. Brower. But . . . approaching him presents some special problems."

"In what way?"

"The change of name is part of a significant pattern. He's very wary. If he suspects any stranger of having a special interest in him, I am afraid he might move on—and be difficult to find again."

"Do you mean he's wanted by the police?"

"He was, for a time. But the charge was withdrawn."

"Aren't you being evasive, Mr. Fergasson?"

Fergasson glanced toward the window seat where Paula was. "It's a rather unpleasant story."

"Miss Lettinger is aware of the infinite capacity of mankind to create unpleasantness. Please continue, Mr. Fergasson."

Fergasson turned some pages in his notebook. "From my previous written reports you know that Mr. Shanley owned twenty percent of an automobile dealership in

Jacksonville, Florida. Six years ago, when he was twenty-eight, he married a woman named Thelma Carr. She had come to Florida to obtain a divorce. Shanley had not been married previously. She was twenty-five, childless, quite a beautiful woman, but without much background. The marriage was a reasonably good one for perhaps three years. There were no children. Then Mrs. Shanley began to . . . uh . . . see other men. Two and a half years ago Shanley followed his wife to an expensive motel at Jacksonville Beach where she had a rendezvous with a man named Jerry Wain. Shanley broke into the motel unit and gave Wain a severe beating. Until the beating Wain was considered a handsome man. He was hospitalized. Due to a severe concussion, he was in a coma for several days. Shanley was charged with assault, but the police could not locate him. As soon as Wain was conscious, he had the charge withdrawn. Shanley reappeared. He made no attempt to contact his wife. He began negotiating the sale of his interest in the agency. While Wain was still in the hospital, in fact the day before his release, a young mechanic at the agency got into Shanley's car to move it to a different parking space to make room for a transport load of new cars coming in. A bomb had been wired to the ignition system. The mechanic was gravely injured. He eventually recovered, but he lost one leg below the knee and lost the other foot at the ankle. That case has never been solved. Shanley sold his interest in the dealership. The day after he sold it, the wife of the young mechanic received a cashier's check in the mail for the exact amount Shanley received, less one thousand dollars. He disappeared at that time."

"Who is this Jerry Wain?" Tom Brower asked.

Fergasson smiled, a thin smile, quickly gone. "A legitimate businessman, he would insist. And present lawyers and accountants to prove it. A few arrests long ago on minor charges, in Philadelphia. I'd say he does have many legitimate business interests. But I would judge that he also is involved in bolita, moonshine, call girl circuits and some discreet gambling clubs. Not as a decision maker or policy maker. An area manager would be more accurate. A showplace home south of Mayport, daughters in good schools, a low golf handicap, a forty-foot cruiser, service on civic committees, regular church attendance."

"Is my grandson still hiding from him? After two and a half years?"

"With good reason, Mr. Brower. Wain has, or had, considerable vanity about his appearance. He had cosmetic surgery done, but the nerves on the left side of his face were injured. The corner of the eye and the corner of the mouth sag. It makes him look remarkably sinister, precisely the impression he has been trying to avoid. My informant in most of this was Shanley's wife. She has not heard from him since he left. They are not divorced. She goes by the name of Thelma Carr." He glanced again at Paula. "She is . . . uh . . . a hustler. She works the cocktail lounges along the beach. She was the one who gave me the details about Shanley, about his hobbies and habits, the details which enabled us to locate him."

"How do you mean?" Brower asked.

"A man can change his name and appearance a lot easier than he can change his areas of interest and proficiency, sir. Memberships, magazine subscriptions, mailorder purchases, these are all . . ."

"Of course. I should have figured that out for myself."

"At any rate, without my having to ask her, Thelma Carr said that Jerry Wain checks with her every month or so to find out if Shanley has tried to get in touch with her. She gave me what I believe is a reasonably accurate direct quote, just as Wain said it: 'A lot of guys are keeping their eyes open, as a personal favor to me, Thelma. Some day I'll find him. And when I do, he's finished.' Evidently this is in the nature of a compulsion with Jerry Wain, Mr. Brower. And I would say that Shanley is aware of this. There is a good possibility they got close to him a year or so ago. He might have been using a different name at that time. I see no point in trying to check it out. I thought you might want to see what he looks like. This was taken with a telephoto lens from a car parked across the street from the used car lot where he works. He is the one on the left, of course."

Paula brought Tom Brower his reading glasses. He studied the picture. His grandson, at thirty-four, was a rangy man, sun-darkened, with a prominent nose, a hard

shelf of brow which shadowed his eyes. His hair was
cropped close and was, in the black and white print,
a lighter shade than his skin. He was turned in quarter
profile toward the lens, wearing slacks and sports shirt
both of vaguely western cut. He was standing with his
hands in his hip pockets, smiling down at a shorter balding man. The smile did not erase the deep vertical creases
in his forehead. There was a prominent cleft in the round
solid chin.

"A Shanley," the old man said wistfully. "No visible
Brower characteristics. No legacy from his mother. You
mentioned his changing his appearance." He handed the
print to Paula. She took it to the window to examine it.

"He wore his hair longer in Jacksonville. And apparently he was heavier and not in as good physical shape as
he is now. Also, his hair was dark then, and it has turned
prematurely grey."

"That's a Brower gene," the old man said.

"He is nearsighted. In Jacksonville he wore glasses
with heavy dark frames. It's a reasonable assumption
he's gone to contact lenses. I do not know whether he
uses tinted ones to change the color of his eyes. Probably
not. I have his address here. Unit 9, Gateway Courts. The
used car lot is called Trade-Way Motors. His personal
car is a three year old station wagon, dark blue. This
information will be covered in my written report. He
seems to live quietly and inconspicuously and alone. I
can't report too much on him, Mr. Brower, because, as I
said, if I alerted him, he might have been gone before I
could reassure him."

"He has a good face," Paula said. "It's a strong face.
It's almost ugly, and yet it's almost handsome."

"He's been in Houston since January. Six months. But
I wouldn't say he's exactly putting his roots down," Fergasson said.

Tom Brower closed his eyes. He sighed. "So what's
the next step? That's why you came here, isn't it?"

"You've never mentioned your plans to me, Mr.
Brower. If it's of any help to you, I tried to ascertain
what Thelma Carr knew of his background. She knew
that Sidney had an older brother named George, but
they are estranged and Sid did not know or care where
his brother was, or what he was doing, or whether he was

alive or dead. She knows he is orphaned. She knows his childhood was . . . unpleasant. She believes he came from Youngstown, Ohio. Perhaps it is fortunate she does not know of your existence, because after Shanley disappeared, some friends or employees of Wain made certain she told them everything she knew. When he disappeared he took his personal papers and records with him. She had never looked at them."

"How does she feel toward him now?" Paula asked.

Fergasson looked at her and with a slight hesitation and faint change of expression managed to convey the impression he thought questions from outsiders impertinent. "I think it seems rather far away to her, Miss Lettinger. She's lived a great deal since he left. And, even in the beginning, I don't think she was a very sensitive or perceptive person. She talked to me because I was paying for her time, and when she ran out of answers, the money would run out. It was that simple."

"Will she tell Jerry Wain someone was asking about Sid?" Brower asked.

"Probably. I represented myself as an insurance adjustor making the final interview before closing the file on the explosion which crippled the mechanic. She had no reason to doubt that. I wanted to find Shanley, I told her, so I could have a terminal interview with him, too. She would not admit that Wain could have had anything to do with the bomb, naturally."

"I want to talk to both my grandsons," Brower said. "I want to talk to Sid first. George can wait. We know how to get in touch with him at any time. But how do we get him here?"

"He might not remember you at all, sir. And if he did, he might not believe you are alive. He might think it's some sort of a trick. It would be expensive, but possible, to just take him and bring him here. But it might easily go wrong. I have the impression he might be difficult to handle."

"I wonder if he would remember this house? He was here for almost two weeks once. It was the only time I ever saw him. He was four years old, and he was a strange, troubled, wary child—with good reason of course."

"If I may make one comment, sir."

"Of course."

"I'm assuming it's your intention to . . . provide for your grandsons. If so, sooner or later, there'll be publicity, because it is a rather large estate. Such publicity might easily endanger your grandson."

"Mr. Fergasson, you are worth even more than the generous fee your agency is charging me."

"Thank you, sir."

"Turn your expense sheets in to young Randolph for approval and payment."

"I took that liberty early this afternoon, Mr. Brower."

"I'm suddenly very tired, Mr. Fergasson. I shall nap and then I shall do some thinking. Please stay at the Inn again tonight, and Miss Lettinger will be in touch with you in the morning."

After Paula saw him to the door, she came back to Tom Brower's bedside. His eyes were closed. He looked as frail and dry as a twist of parchment. His narrow chest lifted with his slow shallow breathing. Thinking him asleep, she wondered if she should leave him in that position, or risk awakening him by lowering the head of the bed.

"The young one is the better of the two," Brower said firmly.

"Is he?"

"You read all the reports on George. Could you imagine George making that gesture of sending the check to the injured mechanic's wife?" His eyes were keen as he looked up at her.

"I guess not. No."

"Sidney—what a dreadful name—is the one worth saving."

She looked at him steadily, gravely. "But who are we saving, Tom, actually? Wouldn't it be you?"

"You're too young to know that much, my dear."

"I'm young enough to wish I didn't. Let's leave it at that. And past time for your shot, by ten minutes. Dr. Marriner will stop by at six, so it's not worth napping until after he goes."

"I'm not tired, except of Adam Fergasson. He has a unique ability to depress me, even when he brings good news. Bring me the boy's picture again. Leave it here on the table where I can look at it."

She fixed the hypodermic, shot the withered, insensate hip, took pulse, temperature and blood pressure and marked her chart.

Thomas Brower put the picture aside and said, "I was sixty-two. It was in the autumn. Jane Weese was a young woman then. She had come to work for me the previous year. Neither of us knew how to entertain a scared child. My dear, go into the living room to the cabinet in the corner beyond the fireplace and see if you can find a small pink box with a carved animal on the lid. It should be on the top shelf."

She returned with it. "This is beautiful work. Is the animal a badger?"

"I've always thought so. It's pink jade, Chinese, very old. Brought back by one of the whalers and traders in the family, from my mother's side, Gloucester stock. I think it might be valuable. I remember a visitor getting very excited about it long ago, but I've never had it appraised." He handed it back to her. "It's nice to hold, isn't it? The little boy fell in love with it. I gave him two new dimes to carry around in it. I gave him the box also. But after his father took him away again, Jane found the box under his pillow. Perhaps I should have sent it to him. I knew where they were at that time. But later I didn't know. I think he must have mourned the loss of it."

"Of course you mean it is the thing he would be most likely to remember."

"You are very quick, Paula."

"You'd send it to him now?"

"What other things would a boy remember? The closest he and I ever got was one warm afternoon in the garden. He was such a remote child, so ready for a blow at any time. That apple tree down in the far corner was old even then. I boosted him up onto that low limb. Has it fallen?"

"It's still there."

"He might remember that. A picture of it. You could take it. And the way the house looks from the road in front, far enough away so you can see the fence. He thought the fence meant it was a jail."

"Poor little guy."

"And then you could take the box and the pictures to

Houston and show them to him, my dear. They could be your credentials."

Her dark eyes went round. "You can't be serious!"

"You have worked over four hundred days without a day off, Miss Lettinger."

"I don't feel abused."

"A change won't hurt you."

"Who will take care of you?"

"Marriner will arrange a replacement for a few days. He'll find some officious biddy who'll irritate me beyond reason, but I'll endure it because I know it will be in a good cause. And no man with a drop of Brower blood in him could look at you and think you were trying to trick him. Can you imagine sending Fergasson down there with the pink box?"

"He'd do it well."

"You can do it better. I don't want that boy scared away. There's less chance if you go."

"I might scare him away, Tom."

"Be careful, my dear. Be careful, but don't take too long. These past two weeks have been pretty good. Too good, maybe. Bring him back with you."

She looked thoughtful. "This is Tuesday. With the best of luck I could leave Thursday. If Jud comes here, he should arrive a week from Thursday, if he comes directly here from Dannemora." She looked at the pink jade box. "It should be time enough." She looked at him with an almost petulant expression. "But I don't *know* how to do things like this. It . . . it scares me, Tom."

"Because you've been making your world smaller and smaller? I have to, you know. Because you want walls around yourself, Paula? Because you got hurt out there?"

"Please, I . . ."

"You haven't wanted any time off. Who is the invalid around here?"

"I've been happy here, Tom."

"Happy?"

"Contented, then."

"A condition, my dear, your paternal grandmother would have thought despicable. She was a hundred and ten percent alive. I just heard the flatulence of Ward Marriner's little red car in the driveway, so you'd better go let him in."

She put the pink box on one of the library shelves, made a face at him and left the room. He picked up the picture of his grandson again. But instead of looking at the picture, he found himself looking at the hand which held it, the ancient hand, a tremulous pallor of lumps and twigs, of spots and stiffness. In that moment it seemed monstrous to him that time should work such a merciless decay. This frail claw had struck blows, hauled lines, lifted weights, caressed the heated sweetness of women long since dead.

He looked through the window, past the wall and the maples to hills turning blue in the shadows of the early evening sunlight. He felt all the weight of a thousand inexpressible regrets, and was afraid he would weep.

"Still with us, you improbable old fraud?" Ward Marriner boomed. "When I retire, I'll look in on you from time to time."

"I'm still here in spite of all the miracles of modern medicine," Tom Brower said tartly. "And you won't live long enough to retire. You're too fat. There's a pretty picture. A fat doctor. Like a bald barber. How do you get in and out of that silly little red automobile?"

"Put this under your tongue, Thomas, and be still."

"Look at the chart, idiot. She took it less than a half hour ago."

"Hmmm. So she did."

two

SID WELLS awoke from an aching dream, his sweat chill in the air-conditioned silence, a memory of his own voice hanging in the room, saying, "Thelma." The dream was gone before he could grasp it, leaving him with a metallic taste, a residue of panic and flight. His phone was ringing. He sat up on the edge of his bed and answered it. It was Scobie, phoning from the lot.

"Sid? Sid, we got a sure thing on that Saab if we pull it down to nine and a half."

"Was Bimmer in this morning?"

"When we opened up, yes."

"So did you ask him?"

"Burnsie did."

"And what did he say?"

"He said it was up to you. The way I see it, Sid, we've had it a long time, you know. I mean you can get sick of looking at something, you keep it around long enough."

"Have you got the card there?"

"Right in front of me, Sid. We allowed eleven bills on it against a Chrysler that went at twenty-two five, and we got three bills out of the Chrysler including the shop order on it. The shop debited us sixty dollars on the Saab. So what that would be . . ."

"It would be taking two hundred and ten off what we cleared on the Chrysler, which brings us below percentage on both of them, Scobie."

"But this is clean, Sid. Cash on the line."

"What do we have to have to make percentage on both?"

"One thousand seventy-five."

"Two months ago, Scobie, you would have apologized and figured it out and called me back."

"I guess that's right. Maybe I'm learning."

"Kid, you can pull it down to an even thousand, and we'll put the plates on it, but that's as low as it goes. Can you deal?"

"I can sure try, Sid. Thanks. I wake you up or anything?"

"I was up. After ten isn't it?"

"A woman was here looking for you. I told her you come on at noon today."

"Buying?"

"I don't know. I don't think so somehow. One thing I noticed, she's driving a rental."

"What does she look like?"

"Not bad. Not bad at all. Medium tall brunette, knocking thirty, stacked pretty good, no wedding ring, talks Yankee, well-dressed. A nice smile, Sid. She didn't give a name. Burnsie asked her. She just said she'd be back is all."

"Scobie, was she a little on the . . . on the rough side?"

"Oh no, nothing like that. More like a lady, Sid."

"Thanks, kid."

He hung up. He took a long shower. As he showered and shaved and dressed he thought of all the things he always thought of whenever something happened which could not be immediately explained. Were they still looking? Maybe not actively, but Wain would never give up. Not with two kinds of pride at stake, the deadened face and two failures on the record. And he reviewed his preparations, looking for a flaw. All proof of his actual identity was in a safety deposit box in a bank in Jessup, Georgia. A detailed search of this motel unit would turn up nothing to tie him to Sidney Shanley of Jacksonville. He always wore the same belt, with a concealed zipper compartment containing the lock box key and two thousand dollars, half in fifties, half in hundreds. He could walk away at any time, leaving behind the car, the clothes, the innocuous belongings of Sid Wells, stroll away, take a bus, take a plane, find a new place, establish a new identity, find work in any city in the country doing the same thing, selling cars to the people. Used cars. Be ready to wander, or be ready to die. He sensed that one day he might lose patience with his own solution to that dilemma. Life, under that discipline, had limited merit.

But for now it was the lesser of the two evils. Stay wary and stay alive, for the meager pleasures of the loner, food and drink, books and walks and climate, the infrequent girl who also wants to avoid emotional involvement.

He arrived at the lot a little before noon. Scobie had unloaded the Saab and was delighted with himself even though, by taking the deal below percentage, he had shorted himself slightly on his commission, and shorted Sid in a very small way on his override as lot manager. Vern Burns was working on a small rancher. Scobie said he doubted Vern and the rancher had said over ten words apiece in the last half hour. They were leaning against the tailgate of the pickup the rancher was thinking of buying, staring out at the hustle of traffic on Almeda. Joselito was working his way along the front line, rubbing the dust from the specials under the striped canopy. A yellow T-Bird turned slowly on the big tilted wheel. The pennants hung limply in the airless heat of July. Inside the sales shack, bright as a fragment of Mondrian, the window conditioner rattled busily. Scobie reported all that Bimmer had said. Sid listened, standing and looking out the picture window, his arms folded.

"I needed that sale," Scobie said. "I was feeling like I was standing in a hole." He was a blonde boy with an understated chin, an earnest, likeable manner.

"You can sell," Sid told him. "When you don't get too anxious, you can sell. And this is a good place for it. There's forty ways to steal, and Bimmer uses only about four of them. So face the folks relaxed. They deal once a year and we deal twenty times a day. Who has the edge?"

"I guess we do, but sometimes I . . ."

"Is that the woman who was looking for me?"

Scobie came to the window. "That's her, sure enough."

She had parked her rental Falcon fifty feet from the shack. His wariness diminished as he looked at her. She looked, as Scobie had said, like a lady. She wore a grey blouse, blue skirt, blue shoes, carried a white purse. She walked well, an erect leggy stride, her head up and shoulders back, squinting slightly in the sunlight as she stared toward the shack.

When Scobie opened the door for her she looked directly and inquisitively at Sid. "Mr. Wells?"

"Yes?"

"I'm Paula Lettinger. I'd like to speak to you on a personal matter, if you aren't too busy right now." Sid glanced at Scobie. Scobie nodded and went out of the shack.

"Will you sit down, Mrs. Lettinger?"

"It's Miss. Thank you."

He sat on the corner of the scarred desk, looking down at her. He held a light for her cigarette. It trembled as she held it to the flame. She was attractive. And troubled. And thoughtful. Suddenly she looked at him very directly and said, "I guess I have to do this my way. I'm no good at tricks. I can't make things up. What you must understand, I mean you no harm."

"What's that supposed to mean?"

"I was told to make up some kind of a story. To get your guard down, or something. I was told that if I came right out with it, you'd run."

"Came out with what? Run from what?"

"You don't look like a man who'd run. But I know you have been running. Please don't run from me. Please give me a chance."

"I don't know what you're talking about. You must have the wrong guy."

"Possibly. I have something with me. I want you to look at it. If it doesn't mean anything to you, I'll go away and I won't bother you any more. But if it does mean something, then we must talk. Is that all right?"

"Miss, you can show me anything you want to. I don't know what this is all about."

She snapped the white purse open and dipped her hand in. As she brought her hand out, he reached very quickly and clamped his fingers on her wrist. He had bent down toward her. Their eyes were close. She looked at him steadily and said, "Don't be afraid of me." He looked at her hand. She held something wrapped in tissue.

"You say wild things, Miss. It's a hot day."

"Unwrap it yourself. It won't bite."

He hefted the small heavy object. He thought of the ways they did things. Not in the daylight like this, not with Scobie and Joe and Burns nearby. He unwrapped it. The pink box and the small carved animal were tantalizingly familiar. His hands had begun to tremble and he did not know why. He opened the box and saw the two shiny dimes, and it all came flooding back, clogging his throat, blinding his eyes. He stood and walked away from her. She said something. He heard the sound of her voice but he could not understand what she said. She said it again. "Do you remember him?"

"Yes. I remember the old man." He stood with his back to her.

"He's dying."

"That old man? He died long ago."

"He's ninety-two. I'm his nurse. He sent me down here to bring you home, Sidney."

He turned and tried to smile at her. "Home? Does he think that's my home?"

"You don't have any other do you?"

He looked out the window. Burns was bringing the customer toward the shack. She said, "There's a lot I want to tell you. And maybe a lot you would like to ask. I'm staying at a motel. The Houston House, just off the Gulf Freeway near the airport. I'm in number ninety-two. Come out there after work, why don't you? And . . . please don't run. It would mean I did it wrong."

He pushed the box toward her. "Take it along."

"It's yours," she said. "He gave it to you a long time ago. But you left it behind, under your pillow. He never thought you meant to leave it."

"A very long time ago," he said. She gave him a brief and uncertain smile.

"I'll wait for you," she said, and went out as Burns and the customer came in. Burns had made a deal. Sid approved it. They left to arrange about plates. Scobie came in and picked up the jade box.

"What's the animal on here, Sid?"

"It's just an animal. I don't know."

"She was selling this junk?"

"Put it down, Scobie."

"Sure. Sure. What are you getting so hot about?"

"Mind the store," Sid said, going to the door.

"You be back?"

"I don't know."

He got into his wagon and drove an aimless mile and found a beer joint he had never been in before. The air was frigid and the juke was noisy. He sat at a table in the back, chair tilted against the wall, hat tilted forward over his brows, thumb hooked onto his belt. The two thousand dollars was there, nested and comforting. Walk-away money. Sid Wells could be laid to rest. Then there would be no need to try to figure anything out, no need to try to judge the woman.

It all seemed too tricky and intricate to be anything except exactly what the woman claimed. It wouldn't be Wain's style. The incident in Atlanta had demonstrated Wain's style. The finger, the confirmation, stealth in the night, and then a sudden dirty violence. Atlanta had proved it was suicide to relax.

And even if she was exactly what she claimed, what did he owe that old man?

But one thing bothered him. How had that old man managed to have him found? How had that old man accomplished what Wain had failed to do? Obviously, he had left some sort of a trail. And if he did not find out what it was, he could not stop himself from leaving it again. She could tell him how it was done. Yet if he went to see her, he might be walking right into a setup.

He decided to see her. Once he had decided, he felt glad. She had good hips and good eyes. She moved well. Woman hips and woman eyes, but the forearm and wrist clearly childish in his memory, a little neatness of pale hair against honeyed skin, and a fragility of bone, and warmth under his grasp when he had touched her, when she had dipped her hand into the purse and the warning bells had rung.

But he would see her with guile and preparation. And no matter what happened, this was the end of Houston. The lair had been violated.

In the late afternoon he went back to the Gateway Courts. Once it had been a transient motel. After a re-routing of a highway, it had been remodeled into small efficiency apartments priced to rent to locals. He parked some distance away and approached in a careful way, a way he had thought out long ago, to a place where he could look, listen, enter quickly and quietly. No one was there. No one had been there. He called the Houston House. Yes, they had a Miss Lettinger registered. Unit ninety-two. She had arrived the previous evening. He phoned Bimmer and said he was quitting. Sorry. Family emergency. He wouldn't be back. Vern Burns could handle the lot. Bimmer was upset about it. He had some money coming. Not very much. Sid told him to mail the check to General Delivery, New Orleans. Small fee for a false trail. He showered, changed to a tropical weight suit, packed his big cheap suitcase and put it in the back of the wagon. He had a few hundred dollars in a bureau drawer, under the newspaper lining. He put it in his wallet. There was no room in the belt. He scrawled a note to the owner saying he was leaving, and sealed it into an envelope with his key. The rent was paid in advance. No bills due. No bank accounts. A utility deposit that would more than cover the reading on the meter.

He looked around the place without pleasure or regret. He felt nothing. It had been another place to hide. Another burrow. When the smell of the predator drifts down on the wind, you dig your way out and go dig another hole to stay alive in. Whether it makes sense or not. Just the stubborn will to stay alive on any terms at all. Or maybe just the desire to frustrate someone who seriously wanted you dead.

As soon as it was time, he drove to the airport and put the car in the parking lot. He carried his suitcase to the cab line and taxied to the Houston House, registered as T. K. Hollister of El Paso, and paid cash for a single night occupancy of number seventeen. He took off his jacket and tie, unpacked a bottle of bourbon, one-third empty, and made himself a drink. He turned the room lights off, opened the door and stood behind the screen, looking out at the warm night. Beyond an angle of one of the wings he could see the lighted pool. A young couple went by, snickering and whispering to each other. Colored floods shone on the shrubbery. He sipped his drink and watched the units across the way until finally a portly couple came out of one of them, locked their door and headed for the restaurant. When they were gone, he wandered over and made certain of the room number. Thirty-four. He went back to his own place, made a fresh drink and called Paula Lettinger. She answered eagerly on the first ring. "Sidney? I was beginning to be afraid you'd . . ."

"I didn't run. Not yet."

"I'm so glad. Are you phoning from the lobby?"

"No. I'm a paying guest too. Number thirty-four."

"I . . . I don't understand."

"Come on around and I'll buy you a drink. We can talk here."

"Well . . . all right. It will be a few minutes."

"I'm not going anywhere."

He went back and stood in the dark doorway and waited. After five minutes two men came along the far walk, moving purposefully. He tensed and felt a coldness along his spine. But they walked on by. After five more minutes he saw her coming from the left. He recognized her when she walked through the glow of floodlights. She wore a pale green dress, carried the same white purse. He heard the tacking of her high heels on the walkway. She was looking at the numbers. She stopped at thirty-four. He thought he could hear her knock. He was not certain. He waited and watched. At last she started slowly back the way she had come. He finished the drink, put the glass aside, walked swiftly and silently across the grass between the wings and spoke her name before she could reach the area of brightness.

It startled her. "Oh. Where were you? Getting cigarettes or something?"

"I just happened to see you. Couldn't you find it?"

"I found it. I knocked and knocked."

"Seventeen?"

"You said thirty-four."

"Did I? I'm sorry. I must be nervous. Come on. My place is over there."

He took her back to seventeen. He held the screen open. She hesitated and walked into the darkness. He went in quickly, close behind her, pushed the door shut, grabbed her shoulder and spun her back into his arms. With an objective and calculating coldness, he watched her and watched himself. She felt sturdier than he had expected, a lot of woman-warmth and resistant fragrance in his arms. She fought him in a dogged gasping silence, wresting her mouth away. He grabbed her dark hair and levered her face back, holding her strongly, caressing her ruthlessly and intimately. Then he sensed that her strugglings were bringing her to the edge of excitement and response. He felt the change in her mouth and in her breathing, and wryly measured his own reaction to that response. She sensed her danger and gave a long shud-

dering sigh and went absolutely limp and dead in his
arms. This was a considerable woman. And a smart one.
He released her abruptly. She staggered and caught her
balance and moved back away from him.

"What do you think I am?" she asked in a rusty indignant whisper.

"That's what I'm trying to find out."

"Turn on the lights."

"Shut up," he said. He put his hand against her shoulder and shoved hard to send her stumbling over to sprawl
across the bed, hissing with alarm. He went to the window and lifted one of the flaps of the venetian blind
and looked across at number thirty-four. He saw no one
anywhere near it. A light went on behind him. He
dropped the flap, put the night chain on the door and
turned and looked at her. She was standing by the bed,
looking disheveled and smeared and indignant. He picked
the purse up, hefted it thoughtfully and took it to her.

"There's the bathroom. Fix yourself up. Stay away
from the phone and we can get along just fine."

She snatched the purse away from him. "Thinking
everybody is an enemy or something! That's paranoid."

"In a foxy world, sweetie, you can get to be a very
tricky rabbit."

She gave him a contemptuous look and swept into the
bathroom and banged the door. He stretched and yawned
with the slackening of his tension. He had wanted to
shock her off guard and watch her response. If it was indeed a setup, she would have responded to him. It would
be expected of her. Fish grab the bait. It would just have
been a little sooner than she would have expected.

When she came out of the bathroom she seemed subdued and thoughtful.

"Bourbon?"

"With a little water, thank you." She went over and
sat at a round lamp table and lit a cigarette, shook the
match out and tilted her head as she watched him. "You
were just carried away, huh?" she said.

"I didn't know what I was doing."

"You knew exactly what you were doing. This whole
thing is very damned devious, Sid."

"I lead a devious life. I was going to run. But I got to
thinking. How did you know I might run? Do you know

what I would be running from? How did you find that
out? How did you find me? After I know those things, I
can run better. I can get the knees higher. A little more
form and a little more endurance. So I think you better
tell me a lot of things, Paula."

She took the drink and sipped it and put it down and
opened her purse. "I'll tell you everything I can tell you,
Sid. Everything I know. But first sit there and look at
these. My Polaroid credentials. Look at this one first.
Jane Weese took it. Do you remember her? She's still
there. I'm standing by Tom's bed. Would you know him?"

"He looks so little. He was a huge man. In my memory,
he was a huge man. He could be any old man in the
world. My God, he looks old. Ninety-two? Does he know
what's going on?"

"Mentally, that old man could take us both on at the
same time. Here are pictures of the house, front yard,
back yard."

He looked at them. He felt a flutter of excitement in
his belly. "That old tree. I remember that old tree."

"You were only four years old, and you were there for
only two weeks."

"Two weeks is a long time when you're four."

"He's dying and he wants to see you, Sidney."

"I accept the credentials. Now I need some answers."
She gave a little shrug of her readiness and acceptance.
She looked at him steadily and then her eyes veered
away. He sensed that her unease was a residue of the
few moments when her sensual response to his casual
roughness had, perhaps, undermined her confidence in an
unexpected way. With that act he had forfeited the
chance of any communion which would be unconditionally mild. There was an edge of awareness, an alertness of the female animal, a concealed aura of speculation.

"How did he find me?"

She named the firm he had employed. "A man named
Fergasson found you. He traced you through Veteran's
Administration records to Jacksonville. He found out
about the agency, and about Mr. Wain and . . . your
wife. That whole mess. He talked to Thelma."

"How is she? It's sort of an automatic question. I

don't care too much. I guess I don't care at all. How is she?"

"Alive and well. She's a prostitute. I guess she works indirectly for Jerry Wain."

"What about Wain's face?"

"He had some surgery. It didn't help."

"And this Fergasson probably did me a big favor, getting everything all stirred up again."

"You don't have to worry about that. He said he was closing out the insurance claim on the bomb thing. He looks like some sort of a clerk."

"How long ago did he start looking for me?"

"Four months ago."

"That costs a lot of money."

"Your grandfather is very anxious to see you before he dies. Then Fergasson found you here and took a picture of you and came back to Bolton with it and showed it to us and told us where you were and what you were doing."

"A picture of me!"

"With some sort of telescope thing, I guess, standing in the used car lot, talking to a customer."

"How did he trace me here, from Jacksonville?"

She frowned. "Maybe he told Tom. I don't know."

"But that's the main point!"

"Don't be angry, Sid. I remember him saying he traced you to Atlanta, and he said something happened there that put you on the run again. He told us you would run if we went at it the wrong way."

"So the old man sent you?"

"I . . . I guess he thinks I can make you understand how much he wants to see you. And he didn't think there would be any danger in it, for you. Nobody has ever come to Bolton, looking for you. And you never told Thelma anything about having a grandfather. Thelma knew you had a brother named George somewhere, but she didn't know where."

"But the old man knows where?"

The woman shrugged. "He was easy to find."

"And now what?" he asked.

She looked at him appealingly. "I love that old man. He sent me to bring you back. I want you to come back with me, just so he can see you and talk to you."

He stood up in his agitation, pacing. "Why should I go see that old man? What did he do for me? What did he do for my mother? My God, I wasn't too young to understand some of it. I figured the rest out later. He passed judgment, didn't he? He played God. He had some money. What was he doing while she was dying? Telling himself he was punishing her?"

She raised her voice. "And who are you to play God and punish him?"

It startled him. He stopped and looked down at her. "What do you mean?"

"Don't you know what guilt is? Haven't you ever felt any?"

"Of course."

"Tom Brower has lived a long time with a tremendous burden of guilt. He denied his only daughter. He lost his grandsons. Maybe he has a compulsion to try to explain himself to you."

"He could never explain it."

"He deserves the chance to try."

In the silence he sat down again, slumped, sipped his drink, glowered into space. After a long time he said, "I'm through here. I have to go somewhere else anyway."

"Please come back with me."

He stared at her with an ironic and knowing intensity which made her visibly uneasy. "All right, Nurse."

"He wants to talk to you and George, and he wants to divide up his money between you."

"That's nice."

"He has two and a half million dollars, Sid."

He stared at her and his dry mouth sagged open and he stopped breathing.

three

HE ORDERED food from the motel restaurant. Steak sandwiches. Coffee. With the making of his decision, he was aware of her relaxation, her mood of celebration, her flushed pleasure in a mission performed.

And she wanted to know about him. He told her bits of it. "After I was at that house about two weeks, my old man came and got me. I guess nobody expected that. Why should he burden himself with a little kid? My grandfather wasn't there. The lady tried to stop him. He pushed her and she fell down. He hustled me out to the car. I remembered I'd left that box under my pillow. I started to yell and beg. He gave me a good thump on the head and shoved me into the car and away we went. I was used to knots on the head. I got them from him and I got them from dear brother George. I was at the end of the list. I had nobody I could kick around. I used to dream about going back to live at my grandfather's house. But he never came and got me again. Where was he when I needed him?"

"He looked for you. He had people looking for you. But he couldn't do as much of that as he wanted. It was thirty years ago, Sidney. Depression. He was fighting for survival. He was trying to hold things together, fight off disaster."

"He survived pretty good."

"He didn't really get out of the woods until about 1939. And he didn't know where you were."

"My old man took me and George to another city. I don't even know where. And he got another woman. I can remember calling her Hilda and getting a good smack across the mouth. I was supposed to call her Ma. We moved again and that town was Youngstown, Ohio. I remember the dirty snow in the winter. The schoolyard was paved with brick. My old man worked at Youngstown Sheet and Tube. He and Hilda drank a lot and beat on each other. When they were like that, you stayed out of the way. When I was nine, George took off. He left. He was fifteen. When I was eleven, something broke and fell on my old man at work and killed him. I couldn't cry for him. Hilda got a good piece of money out of it. As soon as he was buried, she sold the junk furniture and took me to Florida. God only knows why she took me along. She had a ball. I met a lot of brand new uncles I'd never heard about. I woke up one day and she was gone. I tried to hitch back to Youngstown. It was the only place I knew. I made it. They picked me up, made me a ward of the court and put me in a foster home."

"Didn't you tell them about your grandfather?"

"It had been a thousand years since I'd spent those two weeks in his house. I was only four. I didn't even know the name of the town, and I knew he had to be dead by then. I left the foster home when I was sixteen. I looked a little older. I bummed around, went out West. When I was eighteen I got onto one of those magazine crews and learned the hard sell, and found out I could do it. Working my way through college, I told them. I hooked myself on my own story, so I would work a while and go to school for a while. I got a high school diploma and the equivalent of about two years of college before I was drafted. I made platoon sergeant in Korea. I got along well with the lieutenant. Ben Tedds. He had a piece of the dealership in Jacksonville, and we talked about it, and afterwards I went in with him. And met Thelma there. And Thelma met Jerry Wain."

She studied him. "And now you are terribly hard and cynical."

"Don't patronize me. I might be just that."

"How about the money to the man who was injured when your car blew up?"

"I might not make that same kind of gesture now. And he wouldn't have sold his legs for what I was able to give him."

"And you've been perfectly happy to just . . . keep running?"

"And you've never run from anything in your life, Nurse?"

"That isn't fair! It isn't the same thing."

He laughed at her. "So I was on target. Tell me about it, Nurse."

"It isn't any of your business."

"Then you can go back to Bolton by yourself."

She stared at him. "You can't mean that."

"I can make decisions for trivial reasons. Why not? It isn't that important to me. You want it all one way, Paula. You want me to strip while you pass judgment. The hell with that."

After a moment she nodded. "All right. It's a dreary story. I grew up in Bolton. I wanted to be a nurse. I had two years at Syracuse before I went into training. I trained at New York Presbyterian. I met a man named Judson Heiler there. He was brought in with a very bad leg fracture. He'd walked in front of a cab after leaving an advertising agency Christmas party. He was very charming and clever and witty and complex. And weak. And I was very young and earnest and credulous and idealistic and very strong. It was perhaps the world's worst marriage. Worse for him than me, I guess, but I didn't think so at the time. He tried to fight my dominance. I wanted to make him over, make him as earnest as I was. He fought me with women and liquor and unreliability. He kept getting fired. I had to go back to work. Finally, something about my strength or his weakness, made him impotent. And he started writing bad checks. That's a familiar psychiatric pattern, but I didn't know it at the time. I sued for divorce. He got in a few jams and then got a suspended sentence, and then did it again in a big way and got sentenced to five years. The divorce went through. I petitioned to get my maiden name back. I went to Albany and worked in a hospital there. But I was emotionally exhausted. I couldn't endure all the intrigue. Well, over a year ago I heard about Tom Brower. I went home. None of my people are left now. I guess he's my people now. I live in. I care for him. He's paralyzed from the waist down. He's a keen and courageous old man, Sid."

"You found a place to hide."

"If you want to put it that way. Jud gets out next week.

He hasn't behaved well in prison. He served the whole
five years. He hasn't anyone. I've never felt right about
the whole thing. Tom explained it to me. I felt guilt.
Some of it had to be my fault, I guess. Tom made me
come down here to bring you back. I didn't want to do
that. I was afraid. And he made me write to Jud and ask
him to come and talk to me. I didn't want to do that
either. But he said I can't hide from everything. I suppose hiding is a part of running. But you know . . . talking about you, with Tom, neither of us can really understand why you've had to hide. Mr. Fergasson seems to
accept it. I guess it's a part of the world we don't know."

"You think I over-reacted?"

She frowned. "Almost too much melodrama."

"Like a man getting his legs blown off?"

"But after all this time, over two years, two and a half
years, would he still care that much?"

"I spoiled his face. I humiliated him. I put him in the
hospital, and his wife and daughters and social buddies
could read that it happened to him because he messed
with somebody's wife. Nobody has more pride than a
hoodlum. Just as long as I'm walking around, it's a score
unsettled. I guess I wasn't taking it seriously enough in
Atlanta. I was living in a cheap motel. I woke up in
the middle of the night with a headache. Two men had
sneaked in, rapped me on the head, taped my mouth full
of socks, taped my wrists and ankles. They whispered
greetings from Jerry Wain, apologized that they had to
give it to me the hard way, doused me with lighter fluid,
lit me and walked out."

"Dear God!" she whispered and closed her eyes. Her
face was grey and sweaty.

"But they made a little mistake. It was plastic tape.
Heat melted it. They tossed the match onto my legs.
They came loose seconds after my friends left. I rolled
off the bed and dived through the window, sash, glass
and all, and rolled the fire out in the wet grass. It was
raining. The specialists didn't hang around to make certain it worked. They knew it had to work. But it didn't.
A kid untaped my wrists. Firemen put the fire out. I
said I'd been smoking in bed. By dawn I was two hundred
miles from there, and I've been very careful ever since."

"I didn't know it was . . ."

"What am I supposed to do? Go back and talk Wain out of it? Ask for police protection on a permanent basis? What can that wise old man figure out for me, with your help?"

"We thought of one thing."

"Yes?"

"Money can make a hiding place. A private island somewhere. Body guards. Alarm systems. You don't have to be out in the middle of people."

He shook his head. "The mystery man of the islands, his personal radar searching the horizon day after day. Come off it, Nurse."

"Is your way better?"

"I'm alive. Maybe if I inherit money and get my name in the papers, Wain can solve my problems. He can send some friends to kick my spine loose. You see, the unforgivable thing about it, from Wain's point of view, was that it was a woman worth, at the most, a mild argument. She's in the right business now."

"Was she really that bad?"

He held the bottle to the light. "Enough of this and enough of the ice for one more apiece."

"All right. But you might have to help me find my room. Was she that bad, really, Sidney?"

"A week after we were married I began to suspect I had nothing. A man who marries a showcase wife deserves just what I got. She came to Florida to get a divorce. I wanted to parade her around. I wanted the populace to drool. It's a poor basis for marriage. She had the sexiest figure I ever saw. I wanted people to say, "There goes that successful young car dealer and his gorgeous wife." I was climbing, and she was a status possession. A week after I married her, I began to realize that behind all that glandular equipment was somebody I didn't know and didn't even like, a bone-lazy, dull-minded, self-adoring woman. Greedy and empty and sullen. She could spend a whole day fixing her hair twelve different ways, trying on everything she owned, posing for herself and patting herself and caressing herself. She wanted passes made at her. Passes made her feel beautiful. But she was almost completely indifferent to what came after the passes. She could perform adequately, but it bored her. But I couldn't stop wanting

her. I couldn't look at her without wanting her. She
knew it. It was like a sickness. She used it, too, to get
the things she wanted. It started to go sour when she got
bored with getting all her reassurances from me. I knew
she'd begun to roam. I couldn't catch her at it. But I
still wanted her. I had the idea that if I could catch her,
it would cure the sickness and I'd be free of her. I
found out she was meeting Jerry Wain. It took me three
careful weeks to set it up so I could walk in on it. I
caught them at a hotel at Jacksonville Beach. I learned
later he owned a piece of it. It was a Saturday afternoon.
Late. They were naked and a little bit drunk, and she
was performing a little special service for him. When I
came in, she jumped back away from him, her eyes rolling
like a scared horse, and she was making a constant
whining sound. As I was cornering him, I didn't even know
he was hitting me. I didn't feel wild. I just felt careful
and remote and workmanlike. I kept him in the corner
and watched the way his face blurred and split and
changed. I don't know how long. When I let go of him
he just slid down the wall and fell over onto his side.
You wouldn't have recognized him. I squatted and felt
his pulse. When I knew he was alive, I yawned. That's
a funny thing, isn't it? I couldn't stop yawning. I went
to the bathroom door. She'd locked herself in there. I
could hear her gasping and whining and throwing up in
there. I yawned again, because I knew I wouldn't give a
damn if I never saw her again. And I didn't. I knew
Wain had a very quietly rough reputation, but I didn't
think too much about it until that fellow tried to move
my car, the day before they let Wain out of the hospital.
Thelma must make a pretty fair whore. She's got the
build, and the dull mind and the greed. She isn't evil.
She's just a stupid animal." He drank half of his drink
and looked at Paula. She sat with her face in her hands.
"Too much of it?" he asked.

She looked at him. "If you'd just turned around and
walked out."

"I know."

"I'm glad you talked about it."

"I talked too much." He shrugged. "I don't know why
it should make me feel shaky to talk about it. I've never
talked this much to anybody, I guess. I've lived with the

idea Wain wants me dead. I don't want to oblige him. You listen good, Nurse."

"I understand it better." She gave him a strange and twisted look. "Jud would have gotten along just fine with Thelma."

"What do you mean?"

"He loved to say all the pretty romantic words. He loved making poetic statements and little caresses. He could make me feel almost beautiful. But . . . he would have been satisfied if things could have always stopped right there, with just the pretty words and tender kisses. He didn't have much heart for the rest of it." She flushed and got up quickly and went to the window, lifted a flap and looked out. He finished his drink, and went over and stood near her. She looked at her watch.

"Did you know it's after midnight?" she said.

"You've had a busy day."

"What day can you leave?"

"Tomorrow."

She frowned at him. "Don't you have things to do?"

"They're all done."

"And we can fly back tomorrow?"

"We'll go in my car. I don't like to be without a car. Travel any other way and it's too easy to find out where you came from and where you went. We'll drive right on through. You can spell me. Thirty-six hours should do it. On Monday morning old Tom can look at his grandson. I don't know what good it will do anybody. We can pick up a couple of things on the way. Thermos for coffee. Some kind of a rig so the person not driving can stretch out in the wagon and get some decent sleep."

"Well . . . all right, Sid."

"I don't know. The way you can just leave. No roots at all."

"No friends? No woman? Is that what you mean?"

"I've got some acquaintances. I won't be missed. No woman at the moment. No. A pickup sometimes when I get too restless. But I have to get damned restless for that kind of thing. A woman to have for a little while. Sometimes. Not often. Not many."

"It isn't any of my . . ."

"I know that. But you keep asking and wondering, don't

you? You want to know all there is to know. What good
is it doing you?"

"Please, Sid."

"Find a warm and comfortable woman and a safe
place to be with her, one that can willingly accept a
man with no past and no future, one that doesn't have
any need for the kind of emotional security that makes
most of them try to nail you down forever and ever.
One that just accepts, without being either too humble
or too grateful or too indifferent. How many of those
are there?"

"Don't be angry with me. Please."

"Nurse, you found yourself a running animal, but you
want to insist it has no right to be different in any way.
Running isn't supposed to change it at all. You want it
to be just like anybody else, underneath. You want me
to say, Aw, shucks, I'm just a decent fella had a little
bad luck."

"But I don't want you to dramatize yourself either."

He stared at her at close range. She stood facing him,
the light against her cheek and her dark hair. She squared
her shoulders, mildly defiant.

"You're just a messenger, aren't you?" he asked gently.

"I guess so. If you say so."

"How many judgments should messengers have? What
do you represent, Nurse Lettinger? Perfection?"

"I never said I . . ."

"Your kind of running is cleaner than my kind of running?"

"Now really," she said and tried to laugh. He caught
her as she started to turn away, wrapped her in long
hard arms, kissed her mouth as she gasped, held her
through a struggling briefer than before. She went limp
and dead, the defence which had worked before.

He turned her against the wall by the window, kept
doggedly at her, stroking the long firm body under
the thin green dress, searching for her response, de-
manding her response, wearing a cold inward grin as
he felt the tremorous ripeness growing to meet him, then
fading as she forced it back.

This was the humiliation for her, to be forced into a
loveless response, to feel the hidden animal awakening,
to be turned against herself by all the circumstances of

her long hunger, a strange place, drinks, all the emotion and tension of the past hours. Her breath began to whistle with each inhalation, and she began to fight him again, but he knew she had come to that decision a little late. She fought him languidly, like a battle conducted in a dream, her arms soft and listless, her head heavy. He kissed her throat and caressed the good hips and found her lips again. Her mouth broke and searched, and she made a groaning articulation, and arched herself steeply against the wall to press into him. He knew it was won then, unmistakably. There would be other protestings, but he could take it the rest of the way. He could strip her where she stood and carry her to the bed. She knew it too. This was a considerable woman, who could be deeply aroused, and all her responses would be strong.

He released her and backed away and lit two cigarettes. She leaned against the wall, breathing hard, dark hair tousled, mouth smeared, lips swollen. He held a cigarette out to her. She slapped it out of his hand in a small shower of sparks. She walked unsteadily to one of the chairs and sat hunched and humbled, her face against her knees. She rocked her head from side to side.

Finally she looked at him and said quietly, "You son of a bitch."

"We shouldn't get so carried away."

"What does it prove? Why did you have to prove it? My God, you didn't want to leave me very much, did you? You can believe what you want, but nobody ever did that to me before, not like that. Not so cold about it. As if I was watching myself in a sort of horror and not believing it. Do you have to hate everybody?"

"I thought we ought to get something established, Nurse. You're not dealing with a very nice type. You seem to want to think so."

Her face was cold and still. "Why did you quit?"

"Why not?"

"Do you know what you would have gotten?"

"I have the general idea."

She touched her chest with her fist. "About ten percent of me. Just the animal. You probably could have gotten a real big reaction out of the animal, but when that was over, I would have vomited. God *damn* it, Sidney, I'm worth a lot more than that. I'm worth more than being used like a towel. I've got value. I'm worth cherishing. I've got value you could never understand. If you could ever get the whole package, not just that squirmy ten percent, you'd know what I mean."

"It would probably be a lot. Sure. But how about the price tag, Nurse? All the vows, all the pretty words, all the tendernesses it would take to sell you. I just haven't got the time. Or the inclination."

"I know. You're too busy running. You probably take after your father, Sidney. I can understand a little better why Tom didn't want his only child going off with a man like that. Maybe George will turn out to be the better bargain."

"You're very angry, dear. Because I didn't give you a shred of rationalization. I didn't leave you with an excuse."

"Why haven't you asked about George?"

"Because I don't give a damn about George."

"Or about anybody except yourself."

"How can you say that, Nurse, when I'm going all the way up there to see that fine brave intelligent old man? If you don't talk me out of it."

She started to say something in anger and then caught herself. "I keep forgetting I'm just a messenger. Sorry." She got up and picked her purse up.

"Shall I walk you back?"

"Don't bother. Thank you for a miserable evening, Sid."

As he took the chain off the door, he said, "You can fly back. I'll show up. Not as soon as Monday, but I'll show."

She looked at him and looked away. "I'll come with you. I haven't much to pack. We can leave any time you say." He held the door open for her. They said goodnight. She hesitated and looked back at him. "I wonder what you proved about yourself," she said. She went off down the walk. He heard the crisp sound of her heels. All around them the people slept, the cars waited, the stars moved. He shut the door against the rising roar of an incoming jet.

After he was in bed he lay awake for a little while, wondering why he had hurt and humiliated her. She seemed pleasant. And vulnerable.

You keep a door shut for a long time. You are used

to having it shut. And then somebody comes along and pries it open a little way. A draft blows in, and it is cold. So you slam the door. You slam it so solidly people get the idea you don't want it opened again. It can be that easy.

four

GEORGE SHANLEY drove home through the silent suburban streets of pre-dawn San Diego. The air-conditioned Imperial seemed to float in an efficient and ghostly silence. He had a slight headache from the drinks. He had the eight hundred dollars he had taken out of the game in the upstairs room at the Chula Club. He was a heavy balding man who looked ten years older than his forty years. His belly rested comfortably against spread thighs. He wore a black silk suit, handmade shoes, a thirty dollar tie.

He had large pieces of some small ventures, and small pieces of some large ventures, but he had no edge at all in the Chula. He was fronting that one for Sad Frank Lesca. A man without a felony on the books had an easier time with the licenses. Frank had smart people operating it. He wished Frank would let him in for a few points. He wished Liz and his four kids would stay up at Tahoe forever, but spend less money while they were up there, as they had been ever since school let out. If Liz would lose some weight, the heat wouldn't bother her so much.

He wished he hadn't taken such a whipping in the tax settlement last April. He wished Cappy Miller would hurry up and get tired of that girl named Mitz and pass her along. He wished he hadn't let Boardman bluff him out of two pots.

But all the wishing couldn't keep his mind off that strange special delivery letter, and all the implications of it. Nicely typed. Nice paper. Dear Grandson. A grandfather he'd never seen. The old guy had to be twice as old as God. Shaky old signature. ". . . most anxious to see you on personal and financial matters before I die.

41

I shall, of course, reimburse you for the expenses of such a long trip."

It had the smell of money. And if there was any, it came at the right time. People pressuring from all sides. Never wanted to give you any time.

As he turned into the curving mouth of the driveway he flipped the dash switch and the overhead door rolled up and the garage light went on. He put the car away, and walked on into the empty house, yawning, loosening his tie, turning on the lights. Funny how quiet the house could get. It even smelled empty.

He stood in the big living room and looked out at the night. There was a little band of grey over in the east. He was tired, but he knew he wouldn't be able to sleep. The letter from that old man opened a very strange can of peas.

He wandered into his study and turned the light on and called Claude Boardman's unlisted number. Claude answered irritably.

"It's me," George said. "Something bothering me."

"You didn't have your mind on the game."

"Can I come over?"

"Sure you can come over, pal. You can come over tomorrow. You can come over any time after two in the afternoon."

"But I . . ."

"Sleep tight," Claude snarled and hung up.

He sat with the phone in his hand for a half minute. He pushed the cradle and when he got a dial tone, he dialed another number. He counted the rings. On the ninth ring she picked it up and said, "Whuzzawaw?"

"Come on over, Syl."

"Hah? Oh. George?"

"Who else could it be, Sylvia sweetie?"

"Don't get nasty. My God, I was sleeping so hard. What time is . . . George, it's *five* in the *morning*!"

"Call a cab."

"Georgia, baby, please maybe it would be better if . . ."

"It would be better if you turn off that motor mouth and hustle it over here Sylvia sweetie, or you could end up on hard times and bad hours. What was that? What did you say?"

"Nothing. Nothing at all, darling. Should the cab wait?"

"Don't get smartass. Don't push the luck. Use the side door." He hung up and prepared slowly for bed. He started to leave a light on and decided there was enough grey morning light seeping into the room. After he had been in bed about ten minutes, she came in. She was a rangy twenty year old Slovak from the Imperial Valley, with a hard body sun-tempered on the beaches, a mane of coarse-textured pale hair. She wore big black sunglasses night and day. She wore black stretch-pants, a red blouse, her hair tied into a scarf, and she carried a little aluminum overnight case. She glanced at him, moved over through the grey light, put the case on Liz's dressing table and snapped it open.

"Did you latch the door when you came in?" he asked.

"Yes, I latched the door."

"It will hurt your mouth if you smile?"

She gave him a broad glassy grin and said, "I smile because I am so happy every minute of the day." She undressed swiftly and padded into the bathroom. George Shanley waited for her. He wished he hadn't sent for her. He wished it was possible to tell her that the only thing he wanted was a closeness for sleeping, to have somebody there. Sleep came easier when the warmth was there, and it was deeper and more healing. But you couldn't tell anybody things like that. You had to have the reasons they expected you to have.

He talked with Claude Boardman at three o'clock the following afternoon. They talked in George's shabby little office in the Walton Building. Boardman stretched out on the red leather couch. He was a narrow grey man with a small confidential voice. He had been very very big, operating on a top policy level on a national basis. And then the cancer had come and they had started cutting him. They had gone after it three times, and Boardman was waiting for it to show up again, waiting with a sour patience. He was past liquor, women, travel and any participation in plans and operations. He was down to the poker and the waiting, but he knew everybody and remembered everything, and could give advice on delicate matters.

"This is a personal problem," George said. "Do you know about the time, over two years ago, I got asked about my kid brother? He got in a mess in Florida and they were looking for him?"

"You got roughed up a little bit, Georgie?"

"Why should they send silly bastards like that? I told those two everything I knew, which wasn't much, and they thought there should be more, so they bounced me off the walls. They sprained my back and I couldn't tie my shoes for three weeks."

"Indignation, George?" Boardman murmured.

"I should think I'd have a little protection from stuff like that."

"Georgie, you take away maybe forty declared and twenty more under the table in a year, and you drive a big car and have a swimming pool, and you snap your fingers and some broad comes running, but it shouldn't give you very big ideas. In a three billion dollar take, you are a very small time thing, and you have been shot with luck to get even as big as you are."

"Are you sore at me about something?"

"Georgie, you get emotional because you are not very bright. I am putting things in perspective for you. Frank Lesca is worth three of you, and he is also expendable. If it was a supermarket, Lesca would be a clerk in the vegetables and you'd be a bag boy. So don't give me tears about being roughed a little. It's a business risk. Why was your brother so popular all of a sudden?"

"After they sprained me, then they clued me a little. Sid got somebody in Florida sore at him. Not in the business. A personal thing. Sid was in the automobile business, and it was some kind of static about Sid's wife with somebody named Wain."

"I remember it now. He disfigured Jerry Wain. Wain had a try at him and missed, and the man skipped. That was your brother? I didn't connect it up. Wain wanted him on a completely personal basis, and there was five thousand offered for information."

"How big is Wain?"

Boardman turned a grey face and stared at George Shanley. "He couldn't set your brother up without clearing it. And it was a personal matter, and he got it cleared. Shouldn't that answer your question?"

"But just how big is he?" George asked stubbornly.

"Lesca has this one little corner down here. Wain has Florida, Georgia, Alabama and South Carolina. And he has the islands. And once upon a time he had Cuba. Also he is on the big board, representing the southeast. Now what's your problem?"

George wiped his sweaty lip with the back of his hand. "Here's all I knew about the kid when they bounced me around, Claude. I took off from home, that was in Youngstown, when I was fifteen. Sid was nine, I think. Our old lady was dead. We had a step-mother. The old man worked in a steel mill. I went back there when I was twenty-two. I checked around. I found out the old man had been dead five years, and no trace of Hilda or the kid. I didn't look too hard. What was the kid to me? We never got along. Right after Korea, or maybe it was still going on, I'm in the Chicago airport and I hear Sergeant Sidney Shanley called, for him to go to the United Airlines desk. I was killing time. It was him, in uniform. We weren't glad to see each other. We talked three minutes, maybe. He told me how the old man got killed. He told me Hilda ran out on him. I told him I was married and I owned a restaurant in San Diego. Like strangers. He didn't say where he was going or what he was going to do. That was it. He'd grown bigger than I thought he would, and he looked hard as a stone. That's all I knew. Then yesterday morning I got this special delivery letter."

He handed it to Boardman. Boardman read it carefully. "Did they ask you about any other relatives?"

"Yes. I said there weren't any. Honest to God, I didn't think there were. Now this old man pops up. My mother's father. In some place named Bolton. I never saw him, but I think Sid was with him for a little while when Sid was real little. About the time my mother died, and the old man was in the tank for something, D and D probably, that old grandpa came and got him and was going to keep him, but my old man went and got him and brought him back. I was maybe ten years old. I'd forgotten all that. I figured the old grandpa for dead. I couldn't even remember that Brower was my mother's maiden name until I saw it on this letter. I don't even know how he found out my address."

"Next question. What happens to you if Wain finds out you were holding out on him? But there are some assumptions there. That's assuming he never has caught up with your brother, which is a big assumption. And, if he hasn't, that he's still eager. It's hard to stay mad too long. But Wain could stay mad as long as anybody you would ever want to meet."

"I'm wondering about if I go there and the kid brother is there too."

Boardman gave him a deathly smile. "So we are down to a question of loyalties?"

George said hastily, "I told you the kid means nothing to me."

"You want an opinion? If Wain hasn't found him and still wants him, and if Wain finds out you tried to be cute with him and resents it, it would become a policy matter, and Lesca couldn't give you an inch of protection. You could find out how far you can swim with some cinder blocks four miles off Imperial Beach."

"Don't say a thing like that!"

"You're not very bright and you have a nervous stomach, Georgie. I read you before you open your mouth. And don't worry about cinder blocks, I forget the modern improvements. You'd have a heart attack."

"Claude, please, all I want is . . ."

"You want me to find out how things stand."

"I want to go there. Maybe there's a piece of money in it. Even ten would help a lot, with no tax bite out of it."

"You live too big, Georgie. It keeps you poor and jumpy."

"Will you . . ."

"Shut up," Boardman said. He looked at the letter again. He handed it back. "Go away, Georgie. I'll call a friend from here. Go downstairs. Have some coffee. Stop sweating. You smell up the office."

At the door George turned and moistened his lips and said, "Another thing. If there's still that . . . that money for fingering him . . ."

Boardman sat up slowly. "Your brother? Your own brother?"

"But if I got to do it anyway. I mean as long as I've got to do it . . ."

"What you've got, I'd rather have cancer."

"But . . ."

"Get out! Get out!"

The anger tired him. After George left he lay back for another few minutes. He went to the desk and took the small notebook from his wallet. He made a call to Miami. He talked for ten minutes. He made another call to Mobile. He stretched out on the red couch again. It amused him to find he enjoyed having a reason to make some of the careful calls, the kind that would mean nothing to anybody who tapped the line. Even on such a dirty little thing like this, it was good to have a reason.

George Shanley waited thirty minutes before Boardman shuffled into the lunch room and sat on the stool beside him.

"They still want him," Boardman said in an almost inaudible voice. "They missed twice. Wain wants him. Anyway, you're in the clear now. Go see Grandpa. It will be checked out. Maybe somebody gets there before you do. I wouldn't know. If he's there when you get there, the kid brother I mean, and if he should disappear right after you get there, you won't look very good, Georgie."

"But I don't want to be around if there's going to be any . . ."

"You better go see Grandpa. They want you to go see Grandpa. Maybe you can help out a little. I don't know. But they want it to be very quiet. Very quick and quiet and no fuss. Maybe Wain wouldn't want it that way, and maybe he won't find out until it's done. Maybe Wain isn't quite as big as he used to be because he worries too much about his face and about your brother, and he doesn't keep his mind on the operation. Maybe people are a little uneasy about him. So it will be like a favor for a friend, and we'll tell him later. It means no five for you, Georgie, because that was from Wain on a purely personal basis. Cheer up. Maybe you make up for it by getting his share of Grandpa's money. A fellow getting his brother knocked off should get something for his trouble."

"Don't do me that way, Claude. I had to protect myself, didn't I?"

"You're protected."

"Any time I can do anything for you, Claude . . ."

five

ON SATURDAY morning, after phoning her room, Sid walked over with his suitcase and they drove over to the airport in her rental car. She wore the blue skirt he had first seen her in, with a fresh white blouse. She seemed subdued and distant, and he imagined her attitude toward him was that same impersonal approach nurses used toward a patient they did not like. After she had turned the car in, and they had put the baggage into the blue station wagon, they went back to the terminal and had breakfast. He noticed dark smudges under her eyes.

"I'd like to call Tom," she said.

"Can he talk on the phone?"

"There's an extension by his bed. But it doesn't ring there. If he's sleeping, I can try again. It will make him very happy to hear I'm bringing you back."

"And it fills you with joy, too."

"I'm just a messenger. I'm glad I'm able to do what he wanted me to do."

"That's nice."

"If he's awake, do you want to say hello?"

"I don't think so."

"Suit yourself."

"It's a small place. It would go through a little switchboard, wouldn't it? I don't think you ought to be . . . too specific about who is coming back with you."

"It's a small place, and I imagine that everybody in town knows Tom has been trying to locate his grandsons. But nobody would know you've been on the run. Or probably care particularly."

"Try to keep it short and vague."

She looked at him. Her dark eyes were cool. "Anything you say, Sidney. I guess that being nervous can become quite a habit. It's a strange way to live, not trusting anybody."

He stood outside the booth as she made the call. He saw her face in profile, expressionless in waiting, then suddenly warm and softening, the smile curving, and he knew she was talking to the old man. To see her like that gave him a surprising feeling of loss. She had worn that look for him, for a little while. When she came out, her face was still again.

"He's very pleased."

"That's nice."

He went to a news stand and bought a road atlas. She had no sun glasses. He bought her a pair.

As he headed north out of the city on Route 59, she said, "You said we'd have to buy some things."

"We'll get them up the line."

The wagon was heavy and powerful. After it had cooled off, he turned the air-conditioning to low. It had been a long time since he had taken a trip. He liked the feel of the car, the way it snugged to the road at high speed. She sat far from him, looking out her side window at the baked land. The silence between them seemed to be an uncomfortable truce.

He was curious about her driving, so when they reached Lufkin, a little over an hour out of Houston, he had her take the wheel. She was erratic at first, picking up too much speed and then glancing at the meter and dropping back, going into the gentle curves too fast, wandering slightly. But then she found the rhythm of the car and the road. She held the wheel high, her hands clenched at two o'clock and ten o'clock, chin high, lips slightly compressed. He lounged back against the passenger door, elbow hooked over the back of the seat and studied her. The blue skirt was hiked above her knees. Her forearms had that little-girl look. Her breasts were high and firm under the white material of her blouse. The line of her throat was lovely. There was, he thought, something obscurely erotic about an attractive woman driving a big car at high speed, an interest composed of contrast. There she sat, the vulnerable animal, perched on her soft and useful hindquarters, all her flesh humming to the vibration of the road speed, with one dainty foot and ankle urging the hammering ton of metal along. Her face held a gravity and a sadness, and he thought it wasteful that after being shut up so long with the dying, she had lost any flavor of holiday in this long trip.

"I want to say some things without you saying a word," he said.

"You certainly . . ."

"That's two words, and this is something that won't work if we turn it into a discussion group. You just keep driving and you won't be able to keep from listening. Maybe it won't work no matter how I say it. I don't want to make any apology about last night."

He paused and watched her mouth. It looked as if she was going to speak, but then she compressed her lips more tightly.

"I thought about it after you went back to your room, Paula. I wondered why I should have done such a crude and lousy thing. I don't have anything against you personally. This isn't an apology. It's just sort of . . . exploring the things behind it. That means understanding me a little bit. I don't have the instincts of a loner. From my background, I guess I should have. But I've always wanted roots. I've wanted my own people around me. A nest-builder or something. So for over two and a half years I've had to live with the realization that I can't afford roots. In the first year I made a couple of very close and very warm contacts with decent human beings. But I had to fake a history for them. And I had to leave without warning. And it hurt. It hurt like hell. Like tearing out little bits of yourself. From the moment you walked into the shack yesterday, I felt that warmth in you, and I felt my own response to it. You seemed to be a symbol of the kind of thing, the kind of relationship I can't have. And as I felt us getting closer . . . I don't know whether you felt it or not . . . I had to slam the door. I had to do something to make it impossible. I remember part of a college psychology course, about insecure children breaking favorite toys to punish themselves. Okay. I broke any chances we had the first time I had a chance. I know how it made you feel, I think. Cheap and humiliated. I got you heated up when you didn't want to be heated up. The funny thing about it, I knew I could do it. I didn't have any question in my mind. I would have looked like an idiot if I couldn't. I think I was able to because, by then, we were already carrying on a second conversation, aside from the one we were saying to each other. I guess I spoiled things, but perhaps that was the smartest thing to do. I wasn't tracking right. From the moment you showed me that jade box, the whole day was unreal. I can put on an act. Hard and cynical and so on. Probably I've made you believe it. But look. I don't think you were humiliated, and I was the only one there to see it. You're a healthy woman, but if there hadn't been something starting between us, it wouldn't have happened. I couldn't have made it happen. I thought of taking you. Maybe I could have. I don't know. You asked me why I quit. You meant it as a bitter question. I think I quit for the same reason I started, that I sensed a strong attraction and I wanted to knock it off before it got a fair start. I have to protect myself and you, because there's no offer I can make. Okay. Now we have to be together for a time. And I don't want it to be lousy for you. I want you to have a better idea of me, a better opinion of me than what you've got right now. I was an insecure kid breaking toys. And having that jade box appear out of nowhere, I felt as if I'd been turned inside out. I felt raw and scared. I'm still scared. I'd built a pretty good wall and it started to crumble. I don't want the kind of a truce we have right now. I want you to feel better. And I guess the only way you can is if you try to understand why it happened. I've been trying to be honest with you. But nobody knows the whole truth about himself, I guess. All I can do is give you some clues. But now suppose you just keep still and think about it for a few minutes, and then say what you think. I . . . I want you to have a better time than you're having. I think you deserve it."

There was no change in her. She kept the speedometer motionless at seventy. He watched her. She bit into her underlip and began to frown. Suddenly she hit the brakes too hard. He was thrown forward. The car fishtailed, tires screaming. She fought the wheel, straightened it out, pumped the brakes again, then went over onto the shoulder in a rumbling of gravel and cloud of dust, and the big car rocked to a stop, stalling the engine.

She slid over toward him, turned to half face him, put her hands flat against his cheeks and looked into his eyes.

She took the sunglasses off, took his off, stared thoughtfully at him. "Not one full hour of sleep," she said in a husky voice. "Not one. Laying awake there and trying to hang onto the feeling you had dirtied me and you were an evil bastard. Trying to hate you. But I couldn't hang onto it. And I figured it out my way. And came up with the same thing you've said. It was another act of running. So I decided to wait and watch and see if I could find some clue that I was right." Tears spilled out of her eyes. "Damn you, Sid. Damn you! I'm not the enemy. You don't have to try to smash me. I'm your friend Paula. Okay?"

"Okay."

She kissed him on the mouth, her lips as tender as though she were kissing a child. He put his arms around her and held her close. Finally she gave him a little push. "Now you drive. I'm too shaky."

He went around the car and got behind the wheel. In a few moments he had it back up to road speed. He glanced at her. She smiled at him. She settled herself so close to him they touched from thigh to shoulder.

"You know, I certainly didn't get to see much of Houston," she said.

He passed a pipe truck and settled back into the right lane. "No punishment?" he asked.

"What do you mean, Sid?"

"Don't you have to get even a little? Shouldn't it cost me a little more than this? It seems too easy."

She reached to the wheel and put her hand on his for a moment. "The ones who matter punish themselves."

"You're a rare one."

"That's what I tried to tell you last night."

They stopped in Marshall for a late lunch. While he bought a thermos, an air mattress, a pillow and a blanket, she went down the block and bought a pair of slacks, a pair of sandals for driving and, at his suggestion, a warm cardigan. When they made a gas stop at the far side of the city, she went to the ladies' room and changed into the slacks. He had folded the rear seat down, moved their bags to one side, and had just finished inflating the mattress with the air hose when she came walking back across the wide concrete apron toward the gas island. The tailored gunmetal slacks made her look leggier, but did not obscure the tilt and tensions of her hips as she came toward him. He saw her become aware of herself observed, and saw a small constraint. She came toward him, properly aware of self and moment, the lines of her, long and strong and clear, coming near with the heavy brows shadowing the dark eyes, her mouth level with promises, grave with awareness. It was disconcerting to him that all of this could have happened so quickly, and kept happening, changing, growing with each hour of nearness. What had been an irrevocable affront to her pride and dignity as a woman now seemed merely a little awkward hitch, a catching of balance, even a quicker way of knowing. All the wanting was there, but this was not the gross simplicity of lust. This was the complexity of a total involvement, a promise of all the ninety percent she had spoken of. Involvement is the heart committed, in the way of an adult—and with this woman, anything less than that would be worse than nothing. But all he could offer was one small option on despair.

They went off into afternoon, the sun behind them. She looked at the maps. "How are we going?"

"Texarkana, and then if we move east too soon we fight too many hills. We'll cut over on 60 to 51. Up through Cairo, Vandalia, Decatur, angle right on 66, and then take the pikes. Fast and flat."

"I don't want to get lost when you're sleeping."

"I'll mark it out for you when we change."

In a little while she said, "Whatever became of Sid Wells?"

"He was a quiet type. Peddled the cars, ran the lot, wrote the ads, paid his bills. He isn't quite dead yet. I'll kill him off after I unload this car. His name is on the paper."

"What do you do then?"

"Sell the car for cash, find a new city, pick a new name, start picking up the little bits of paper a man has to have. Write myself some predated references and weather them up a little. They never check. Avoid the outfits that want to bond you. It isn't hard."

"You talk as if you won't get any money from Tom."

"I might get it. But I might not want to show up to claim it."

"Would you try to change your looks again?"

"Again? Oh, you mean the change from Jacksonville. I was getting too heavy. A little soft. Wore my hair a lot longer."

"Do you wear contact lenses now?"

"No. There was a fair amount of correction in the lenses. It bothered me for a couple of months, being without glasses. Then it stopped bothering me. I think my eyes adjusted some. Things are hazy way off, but not enough to matter. I think Wain could walk right by me on the street. I mean, I like to think he could. I'm not about to test it."

"Nobody should have to *live* that way!"

"Go to any big city at random and go up behind ten strangers, one after the other, and clap them on the shoulder. One out of ten will try to run right up the side of a building. When somebody wants you dead, you make a choice. You kill, or you run, or you build a fort, like Trotsky. Anyway, save your indignation. Name somebody with complete freedom of choice. I feel sorry for myself, but not all the time. I'm alive. I'm healthy. I can make a living anywhere I go, a good living."

"So can a nurse," she said thoughtfully. "Not a good living. But get along."

In a little while she began to yawn. He stopped and she got into the back. He'd arranged the bed on the right side of the car. He found he could sit tall and get a quick glance at her. When he was up to speed he said, "How is it?"

"Golly, it's awful jiggly. Like some kind of therapy."

"Will you be able to sleep?"

"I don't know yet."

A few minutes later there was a sudden warmth of her breath against his ear, a nearby fragrance of her hair, a hand light on his shoulder. She was kneeling behind him. She kissed his cheek. "Thanks for not letting me be gloomy, Sid." She chuckled deep in her throat. "That damn thing will jiggle me to sleep if it doesn't get me too excited first."

"Think pure thoughts, Paula."

"Are there any other kind?" She patted his shoulder and stretched out again. He smiled. Her bawdy little remark had been another peace offering, and a token of trust that he would not take it in any sense of offer. And it also told him something important about her. To be truly desirable, he had learned, a woman has to have a quality of animal playfulness about her sexuality. The broody ones who try to make of it a dark and solemn magic are trapped by their own dramatics. She would have that too, but at the right time and right place. The essential woman has the wisdom to know that it is a romp, a joy, a play, a game for grownups.

When he looked back at her again, she slept there in sweet trust, prone, her hands wedged under the small pillow, face turned away from him, long legs sprawled at rest. The sun was low when he went through Texarkana and headed northeast on 67 toward Little Rock.

When he pulled into a service complex on the far side of Little Rock and stopped by the pumps, under the night glare of the white fluorescence, she sat up slowly, blinked at the glare, arched her back, screwed her face up and stretched and yawned with lioness luxury.

"Sleep all right?"

She got out of the car and reached in and got her purse. She pawed her hair back and looked at him with slightly puffy eyes. "Talk to me before I'm awake and I bite." She went trudging off in search of the ladies' room. She came back with her hair tidied and wearing a fresh mouth.

"I slept like a bear in January," she said.

"We can leave it here and go across to the restaurant. The man says it's okay."

"Can we keep going a little while until my stomach wakes up, too?"

"Sure."

"Should I drive now?"

"After we eat."

Thirty miles further he found an attractive roadside restaurant. It was almost empty. They had a corner booth. After the waitress had gone off with their order, and with their thermos to fill it with coffee, Paula leaned toward him slightly, smiled in an odd way and said, "The invisible man."

"I beg your pardon?"

"You're big. You have a very strong face. You can look terribly impressive and important. But in public places, you blur somehow. I saw it in the airport. You sort of fade into the scenery. It's quite a trick. And I don't want you to be like that."

"After I worked so hard learning how? I studied the kind of people you never really see. They move slowly. They speak just loud enough to be heard. They never change expression. They never look at people. They act as if they are tired all the time. I worked at it a long time. Now it's habit. If you overdo it, you look furtive and people notice you. The easiest way is to pretend you're exhausted and you have a headache. I won't have to work so hard at it while I'm with you. They'll look at you. They won't remember me. I could walk in on my hands. They wouldn't see me."

"Idiot. I'm really quite a plain woman."

"You don't realize how that rubber mattress has changed you."

"I knew *something* was different. I was whistled at. Back at the station. A very small dirty little man. And a very small dirty little whistle. But I've been bursting with morale ever since." Her expression changed suddenly. "It's so strange and so unreal, floating through the night past all the towns and the people on that mattress. Nobody knows where we are or who we are. Like a little dark boat in the middle of a dark ocean. I never had such a feeling of anonymity."

"That's the feeling of running."

"Are we running? That's strange. Now I'll be looking over my shoulder."

"Not while we're running. After you stop, then you get back the habit of looking behind you. When you stop, they can catch up."

"You've traveled like this before?"

"Yes."

"With a woman?"

"A very rough woman. A very dangerous woman. Miss Dexedrine. She can keep you going for forty hours before you fold."

"But she wasn't much for conversation."

"She had me talking to myself."

They ate and went back out to the car. He explained the route. He got into the back, took his shoes off and stretched out under the blanket. The car held at cruising speed. The pillow had caught a slight fragrance of her hair. He looked up out of the window at the motionless stars. He heard little songs and rhythms in the drone of tires and engines. When he closed his eyes he could see her face very vividly and distinctly, looking at _him_ across the restaurant table.

six

THE EXECUTIONER stood at the bar of a roadhouse on Route 5 between Albany and Schenectady, nursing a bottle of ale. He was a stocky, sturdy man in his forties, with light brown hair, pale eyes, and a broad, ordinary, unremarkable face. He wore a grey summer-weight suit which needed pressing, a blue shirt, a maroon tie with a soiled knot. He wore a cocoa straw hat pushed back off his forehead.

He stood and wondered how far away this one would be, and how long it would take. He wondered if this would be the one that turned out to be one too many.

At exactly nine o'clock he picked up his change and walked out into the dark parking lot beside the building. His small dark car was parked at the far end of the lot, away from the others. He unlocked it, got in, reached deep under the dash and pulled the small handgun free of its retaining spring. He put it in his lap and made certain the bulky silencer had not worked loose. He rolled the window down and blinked his lights on and off again, briefly, and sat and waited. Soon a man came walking across to the car. He came up to the window. He looked young and nervous. The man behind the wheel did not like them young and he did not like them nervous. "Jones?" the young man asked.

In the cover of darkness the man held the weapon aimed at the middle of the pale blob of face. "What's the name of Lanti's wife?"

"Huh? Oh, her name is Bernajean."

"Come around the back of the car and get in beside me." As the young man went around the car, the man behind the wheel tucked the gun under his left thigh. As the other got in, he said, "Don't tell me your name. I don't want to know your goddam name and I don't want to see your goddam face."

"Sure. I understand."

"Now tell me about it, and if any of it is guesswork, leave it the hell out because I don't want to be confused."

"It has to look like an accident."

"The rate just went up."

"Where he'll be, if he shows, is in Bolton, New York. It's a small town. It's north of Syracuse someplace."

"An accident in a small town? The rate just went up again."

"His name is Shanley. Sidney Shanley. He's about thirty-four, thirty-five."

"He expecting it?"

"Yes. For a long time. A couple of years anyway. They haven't been able to find him."

"Oh fine! The rate on this one is going to make a record. Has anybody had a try at him?"

"Twice. And they missed twice."

"Bodyguard?"

"They say probably not. The reason he could show up at Bolton, there's a grandfather there, Thomas Brower, and the old man is dying, and maybe there's some money. Maybe he is going to show up, and maybe he has been there all along, at least for the past year. I brought a newspaper picture of him. It's over two years old."

"Bring it out of that pocket an inch at a time, friend, and lay it down on the seat between us. That's nice. You did that just right. What's the timing?"

"As quick as possible."

"But he might not show up at all?"

"That's right."

"Let me think a minute." The young man stirred restlessly in the long silence. Finally the executioner said, "I wouldn't try it for less than twelve five."

"Jesus, that's a lot of money."

"You get sent here to tell me *your* opinions? You bring me a message from somebody I'll never know, and you take one back. That's all. Take back my message. I just don't want this one very much. I just don't like the sound of this one. If he doesn't show, I'll settle for the down payment, which will be twenty-five hundred."

"Twenty-five hundred for nothing?"

"You're all mouth, boy. Here is a little piece of paper for you. Call the number on it at exactly eleven. I'll say Jones and you say yes or no. If you say no, we both hang up. If you say yes, I'll tell you where to bring the down payment."

"All right. All right. Jesus! Like a spy deal."

"Sonny, I'm alive. I've been in business twenty years. Now get out and shut the door."

As the car door slammed, the man started the car and drove out of the lot. He turned on his lights as he turned into the stream of light traffic, too far away for the man to attempt to read his mud-smeared plates. He slipped the gun back under the retaining spring. He drove two miles. He stopped at another bar, ordered another ale, kept himself to himself, his face bland and closed, his big freckled hands at rest. The answer would be no. He was certain of that. And he had pegged the fee at the exact point where he could be indifferent as to whether the answer was yes or no, risk and profit balanced precisely. The minimum risk venture would be an unsuspecting victim in a big city with no stipulation to make it look like an accident. Poke the shotgun through the kitchen window and drop him between the sink and the stove. But there would be no contracts like that for a specialist. Crude labor could handle those at minimum fees. Ignorant expendables. One did not hire a hydraulics engineer to unstop a drain. Also, he could be contacted only through the highest level, and that, in itself, kept it limited to problems beyond regional disciplines.

At eleven, over a pay phone, the answer was yes, and he set up the contact in the same place, in the same manner as before, took the money, drove away. He would never know who had hired him, just as they would never know the day-by-day identity of the specialist they had hired. He would not know why this Shanley had to be taken. That was of no interest to him. It was an assignment. A contract, a problem requiring care and planning in the solution. The target was wary. It would require extreme care.

By the time Jones had driven back to his home in Troy, he had reverted to the habits of mind and the attitudes of his everyday identity, wherein he was Eldon Bertold, proprietor and sole employee of the Harbor Stamp Company—Appraisals, approvals, cash for collections. He rented half of an old house in a defeated section of town, and lived alone there. There was a sidewalk entrance to the tiny shop, a bell that jangled when anyone walked in, and a dusty confusion of stock books, albums, and all manner of philatelic supplies. Behind the shop were many rooms, and over the years each had become adapted to its own special purpose. Most of his stamp business was conducted by mail, and one room was the office where he prepared the approval cards and sheets for mailing to the list of customers he had developed over the years, kept his customer files, and typed his correspondence on the cheap buff letterhead. There was a sorting room with big tables where he made his appraisals and where he dismantled the collections he bought at auction or by direct purchase—throwing away the junk items, transferring the rest to his stock books or approval inventory and, very rarely, finding an item for his own private, specialized collection of United States Issues prior to 1900. He worked upon his own collection in another room, mounting there the prize-winning displays he took to conventions and exhibitions. The rare issues were in excellent safe-files, and on the walls were the framed photographs of special issues and special displays. A glass case held the awards he had received. There was another room, small, cluttered with equipment and lighting fixtures in which he took his superb macro-photographs and slides of rare issues, using bellows and clamps and special lenses on an old Hasselblad. Adjoining his photolab was his converted darkroom.

The kitchen, bedroom and bathroom were in the rear of the house. He had a few cheap clothes, a supply of simple foodstuffs. He put his car in the garage behind the house and went in through the kitchen. He went directly to the room containing the safe files, turned the combination dial on the heaviest one, opened the bottom drawer, removed a tin box from the rear of the drawer and placed it on the nearest table. Under the hooded lamp he counted the money that was in the box, counted what he had been given, put half of the advance payment in the box and replaced it in the bottom drawer of the file.

With a feeling of impatience and excitement he sat down with a note pad and the catalogue of the public auction to be held during two days in August in the rooms of one of the better New York City auction houses. He had previously listed the items he was prepared to bid on, and the maximum bid he was prepared to make on each one. He was weak on the 1857 issues on cover, particularly the various shades of brown, red brown and orange brown on the five cent denomination. They were so rarely included in auctioned collections he had wished he had more money available for this one. Now he could expand his bid list and his alternate list.

He studied the catalogue description of one cover: "5¢ Indian Red (28A). Tied Philadelphia pmk. on cover 'pr. Arabia' to Nova Scotia, 5 transit mark, backstamped Boston Br. Pkt., Halifax Receiving Mark, Fine." He looked at the catalogue photograph and wished he had the original print to study with a magnifying glass. Finally, with all value factors clear in his mind, he wrote the catalogue number and his maximum bid for that item, $215. He turned to the next page . . .

At two A.M. he suddenly realized he was hungry and was still wearing his hat, tie and suit jacket. And he realized that his desire to acquire the items at the auction in August was distracting him from the problem at hand.

He changed to an old bathrobe while the can of pork and beans was heating. The Shanley job, if the man appeared at all, would be delicate. Bolton was not a commuter town for a larger city. It was too far north of Syracuse. Strangers would be noticed and remembered. Conversely, you could expect the police work to be skimpy and clumsy.

When they wanted an object lesson, it was much easier. You come into town. You establish the movement pattern of the target. You fit yourself inconspicuously into some portion of that pattern, selecting the optimum time and place, and the best weapon of opportunity. Then, in a fractional part of a second, you earn your money and walk away from it. Method is of greatest importance.

The F.B.I. statistics show a running count of thirty-five murders a day. Eldon Bertold estimated that thirty-four of them were amateur, beneath contempt, crimes of passion and crimes caused by fright and crimes by people of unsound mind. Of the remaining three hundred plus each year, of the murders reported as murders rather than as accidents, possibly twenty to thirty were professional. The others were committed by amateurs with a certain amount of guile and talent. Of the professional kills that were reported, more than half were certainly at the hands of cheap blasters. And so, weeding it down to the small core of genuinely competent work, he estimated that the true professionals of the trade probably accounted for ten reported and ten unreported kills per year. Of these twenty annual victims, the majority were probably aware of danger—thus indicating the need for expert handling. Shanley was aware that it was not to be reported as murder. He counted back. This would be the sixth . . . no, the seventh accidental death he had arranged. They were easier in an urban environment. In Birmingham in 1953, it had been the easiest one of all. The man had tripped and fallen under the rear duals of a transit mix truck. In Miami in 1957 the man had walked out onto his private dock, boarded his cruiser and tried to start the engines without checking the bilges or starting the blower first. A careless habit, when there might be a quart of gasoline in the bilges creating a vapor as explosive as a sizable charge of dynamite. In Michigan in 1958, if the private plane hadn't burned when it struck, they might have found the wad of waste that had gotten into the gas tank somehow. The easiest pattern in a mechanized society is through the machines for transportation. Man is frail at high speed.

As he went to sleep, he aligned all aspects of the problem in his mind, knowing that in this way, more often than not, he would awake with the beginnings of a plan of action. He tried not to think of the other items he could not make bids upon, and how well they would go with the 10¢ greens, the 12¢ blacks, and the superb 24¢ lilac greys. He tried not to anticipate how it would be, going to the desk, paying the money in cash, walking out with the precious bundle. No other excitement in the world could match that.

It gave him a feeling of ironic satisfaction to realize that the killing had begun, actually, because of the stamps. And, to be fair about it, the fluency of his German had also been a factor. The German had been responsible for his being taken out of the line organization after basic training and ordered to Washington in 1942. After he had passed all their clearances and all their physical and psychological tests, and undergone all their highly specialized training, they had sent him to the unit based in London. Even then there would have been no killing, at least none on a specific assignment basis, had it not been for the stamps, for the alertness of the colonel in command in seeing how splendid a cover story could be fashioned of these materials. They provided him with a compact and valuable collection, gave him new identities and sets of forged papers, sent him in turn to four supposedly neutral countries as a young stamp dealer who had escaped from Germany and was trying to convert his valuable collection into gold or gems. In this way he made contact with those other imitation refugees who were in actuality key espionage and propaganda agents for the Reich. He was provided with special weapons, objects that looked innocent yet, when properly used, were incomparably deadly. During two years of under-cover duty, he executed exactly one dozen, eleven men and one woman. In London they had told him it might disturb him to do this sort of work. One could never tell beforehand. One had to try it and see. He expected it would bother him.

But after the first one, in Barcelona, he knew he would be all right. The victim sipped the scalding coffee, low-ered the cup carefully, stared at Bertold with an odd intensity, as though about to ask a question. Abruptly the eyes lost focus and the single spasm twisted the face out of shape. Then there was the unmistakable slackness, oddly like a still photograph of someone asleep.

He felt no pleasure, no concern, no regret. One less adult human animal in the world, and there seemed to be so many of them that the loss of one was infinitesimal. The business of the woman bothered him slightly. He dreamed about it once. And he remembered her after he had forgotten some who came later.

After the killing was over, he was sent to Germany,

on special duty with the military government, translating, interpreting security clearances. There he met Silvana. On the only night in his life he had ever gotten drunk, he told Silvana what he had done. Silvana said later he had talked quite a lot about the woman. Lieutenant Silvana did not talk about what he had done in civilian life. He was older than most lieutenants. Bertold understood that Silvana had been in city government somewhere in California. When Silvana had paid him an unexpected visit in Troy, New York, in 1946, Bertold's mother was still alive. He was living with her in that same old rented house and trying to build up the stamp business. But he had begun to think he could never get enough return out of it. Silvana paid him five thousand dollars to go down to Mexico City and quietly kill a man named Kelly who, as an employee in charge of a smuggling operation, had developed a nasty habit of hijacking organization merchandise from time to time.

Bertold went to Mexico City, located Kelly and learned some of his habits. Then he bought an ice pick in one store and a file in another. The ice pick had a round wooden handle about the size of a golf ball. He cut the metal down to a two inch length and sharpened it. When he closed his fist around the ball, an inch and a half of metal stuck out between his second and third finger. He went to the bull fights on Sunday, in a loud shirt and a straw hat, with a cheap camera hung around his neck. When the last bull was killed, the crowds moved slowly, tightly packed, through the narrow cement tunnels. He moved in behind Kelly and his group. He was pressed against Kelly. In the darkest part of the fifty foot tunnel, masking his motion by making an awkward show of getting his camera strap off, he punched Kelly solidly, high in the nape of the neck, at the juncture of neck and skull. The compacted throng shuffled a dozen feet further while Kelly was slipping down. Bertold forced himself a little to one side. He began to hear the shouts behind him as others tripped on the body and were forced along and fell. Soon he was in the sunlight. He dropped the weapon down a storm drain. There was a small item in the English language newspaper the next day saying that an American resident named Kelly had died of a cerebral hemorrhage while leaving the bull ring. It said he had

been the local representative of an import-export firm
with offices in St. Louis.

Now Silvana was dead too. And Bertold lived alone
in the house. When Silvana had learned he was dying,
he had set up another method of contact. Bertold's business mail came to a post office box. He maintained a
smaller box nearby under the name of K. Jones. He went
to the post office every day. He always glanced into the
other box. The only letters he ever found there were the
ones, unsigned, which merely gave the date and time and
identifications for someone to meet him and explain an
assignment. Silvana had apparently made his stipulations
clear. Careful contacts. Jobs one man could handle. Top
rates, with a substantial down payment and the balance
on completion. And, in the event anything ever did go
wrong, there would be absolutely no way to trace the
connection back through to the people who paid so well
for the service. Once it had almost gone wrong. The
woman had appeared at exactly the wrong moment, out
there in Minneapolis, and she had given the police a very
good description, so good that even with all the methods
of travel he had used, they had traced him back to
Troy. But there they had lost him. As they had no reason
to assume he had stayed in Troy, he decided it was
safe to stay. But he felt uneasy until, two years later, he
saw a small wire service news item datelined Minneapolis, saying, "Eye witness to the Keogh murder, Hazel
Vanichek, age 31, was fatally injured last night when
struck by a stray bullet during an attempted holdup of
the Plantation Club where she had been employed for
the past year as a hat check girl. The holdup man, Rich-
ard Paris, age 19, was taken into custody in the parking
lot of the club after having been felled by a bullet in the
left leg fired by Detective Lucas Cammer of the City
Police, who was in the club at the time of the holdup
attempt. The Vanichek woman, struck in the chest by the
38 caliber bullet, was pronounced dead on arrival at
City Memorial Hospital. Paris, running from the club,
turned and fired in the direction of Lieutenant Cammer
who was in pursuit of him. Hazel Vanichek will be remembered as the eye-witness to the shooting of Abner
Keogh on June 20th, 1951, at his hunting lodge on Rum
River near Mille Lacs Lake, shortly before Keogh was to

be recalled to give additional testimony before the Grand
Jury in connection with a gambling probe. She was held
in protective custody as a material witness for over
seven months following the shooting, and was released
when all leads to the possible identity of the killer were
exhausted."

It had been simple carelessness. He had known the
lodge had been empty for three days. He saw Keogh
arrive alone. He had assumed Keogh would either bring
the girl, or she would be along later. He had not realized the girl had arrived earlier that same afternoon,
sometime during the one hour he had not had the lodge
under observation, had shut her car in the garage and
gone in to take a nap while awaiting her middle-aged
lover. Thinking the place empty and wanting to get it
over with before the girl arrived, he'd gone in quickly
through the French door he had previously jimmied and,
in the instant Keogh turned, before he could speak,
Bertold had put three small slugs into the meat of the
man's chest, high and just enough off center to the left.
(At the school in Washington, long ago, they made you
fire unaimed shots at surprise targets until, finally, it
became as simple as pointing your finger.) Keogh fell
solidly, dying as he went down, the impact bursting the
air out of his lungs with a mindless retching sound. And
the girl ran out of the bedroom into the short wide hallway, stared at him and ran back in again and snapped
the bolt on the heavy door. Bertold went out of the
lodge at a dead run and stopped at a point where he
could see the bedroom windows without being seen. First
she would try to phone. There was an extension in the
master bedroom. He had removed the units from the
mouthpieces during his inspection of the inside of the
lodge. He reviewed the advantages and disadvantages
of killing her. She had seen him for a few moments in
reasonably good light, but she had never seen him before, and he looked very ordinary, and few people could
give good descriptions. He circled the lodge in the opposite direction, yanked the distributor wires loose on
both cars and began walking swiftly across rough country toward the main highway. He dropped the gun into the
heart of a hollow rotten tree and put the canvas gloves
under a wide flat stone in a creek. He recovered his suit-

case from dense brush near the highway. He abandoned his junk automobile near Milaca, walked into town and had a four minute wait before hailing the bus to Duluth. It was on schedule.

Carelessness, he thought. The girl had recorded him like a camera. Shanley would be as wary as Keogh had been. And his reflexes were probably much better. Keogh had taken a risk because he had thought the girl worth a risk. And had his oyster white silk shirt stapled into his chest by three bullets within a diameter no larger than that of a coffee cup.

He mentally reviewed the information about Shanley. Sleep took him.

seven

THE SUN WAS HIGH. Tom Brower studied his younger grandson. "My dear boy, at ninety-two one wishes to conserve the smallest effort, even that of keeping one's head in a slightly awkward position. So if you would move to the right end of the window seat?"

"Of course."

"And tilt the blinds so I am not looking at a silhouette. Thank you. Sidney, you are a mature and rather imposing looking fellow, in a certain craggy and impassive way. As a small boy you had a very . . . gentle face. Withdrawn and wary, but gentle. Do you remember the house?"

"More than I thought I would, sir."

"Your presence must be due to considerable tact on Miss Paula's part."

"And the jade box. Without that I couldn't have bought it. Without that the whole thing would have been too far out. The box made the connection."

"Did you leave it behind on purpose, Sidney?"

"I forgot it. I remembered it when we were getting into the car, but he wouldn't let me come back."

"I want to ask questions, many questions, but inasmuch as I tire very easily these days, I prefer to use the time telling you about . . . my contemptible part in the first years of your life."

"I don't blame anybody for anything."

"Not consciously perhaps. I shall not embroider this narrative. My only child, Alicia, was born in 1900. She was very like her mother, sweet, vague, imaginative, and not physically strong. I was thirty when she was born, and Margaret, your grandmother, was ten years younger. It was a difficult birth, and a full year before your grandmother was herself once more. As a small family of three, we had nineteen marvelously happy years, though my wife's health was failing toward the end of that time. When Alicia was nineteen she met and fell in love with Clyde Shanley. In those days it was still possible for people to talk about marrying beneath one's self. Shanley was completely impossible. He had no background. He was a strange, violent, bitter young man, given to strong drink and strong language. But he had a kind of wild and reckless gaiety and, for Alicia I suppose, a raw charm unlike anyone she had ever met before. When she persisted in seeing him, in direct disobedience of my orders, her mother and I took her on an extended trip. We had to return prematurely when my wife became less well. Alicia was twenty when we returned to this house. I thought she knew the seriousness of her mother's condition. Two weeks after we returned she ran away with Clyde Shanley. Her mother's condition worsened. I blamed this upon Alicia's cruelty and thoughtlessness. I was a harsher man forty years ago, my boy. Margaret became bedridden. I learned Alicia and Shanley had been married. I should have gone after her then. Perhaps she would have come back. I think that by that time she knew she had made a mistake. I had the fatuous idea she would come crawling back, begging forgiveness. I forgot, or ignored, that terrible pride of hers. I can give Shanley credit for one thing. We were reasonably well off in the twenties, but he had not married her with the idea of receiving monies from me. She wrote us some letters. I did not answer them. I did not let my wife know I had received them. Ah, I was a righteous man, puffed with my own sense of injured self-importance, quelling any feeling of love and sympathy as being a kind of weakness.

"Your brother George was born in 1921. Shanley was moving from job to job, from one industrial city to another. He was a brawler, and found it difficult to keep any job very long. I knew it was only a matter of time until he abandoned my daughter and my first grandson, and then she would come home. I would wait. I lost track of them entirely in 1925. I could have instituted a search, but I thought that would be a sign of weakness. You were born in 1927, I learned later. This was a bleak unhappy house, Sidney. Quite suddenly the world moved into a monstrous era called the Depression. No values were ever the same again. All the security I'd worked for, it all crumbled away, boy. Margaret died in her sleep in 1930. Jane Weese came here to take care of me and the house. I was sixty years old, and I did not give a damn. I was certain I would not live long. I was going through the motions of trying to ward off the ultimate financial disaster, because that was habit, the familiarity of things to do. In 1931 I received a phone call. Your father was in a city jail serving ninety days. Alicia had died after a long illness. They found my address among her papers. Your father's term still had a few weeks to run. I peddled some jewelry that had belonged to your grandmother in order to get the extra money to go there and bring my daughter's body back for burial here. I brought you back too. I would have brought George back, but I could not find him. Two weeks later your father came storming in here when I was out. He pushed Jane to the floor, grabbed you and took you away. I knew that a man like that should not, could not have custody of you. I would take you and George away from him, legally. But it costs money to accomplish such a thing. And I set about my work with a new goal, Sidney. But they were black years. It took time. So much time. I made mistakes. It was almost eight years before I reestablished myself. It took time to get information about you. I learned that Clyde Shanley had been killed in an industrial accident in Youngstown. I learned he had married again. My people could not trace the woman. Where were you?"

"I was eleven when he died. George had run away two years before that. Hilda got some money when my father died. We went to Atlantic City. When the money was gone, she took off. I was twelve. I hitch-hiked back to Youngstown because, I guess, that was the place I remembered best. They picked me up after I was there about three days, and the juvenile court put me in a foster home. It wasn't too bad. They, the couple who took me in, usually had three or four kids at all times. It was a business deal, extra income for sheltering kids."

"We'll talk more, Sidney, later on. I've gotten too tired. Every part of this mechanism is ninety-two years old, full of flaws and fragilities. I'm a passenger in a rackety old vehicle, and I must not force it beyond its limits. But I want you to know I am ashamed of myself, Sidney. A large segment of my life is shadowed by an attitude I now find despicable."

"What else could you have done?"

"Come now, my boy. Don't try to present me with ready-made rationalizations. Out of pride I suppressed my love and denied my only child, giving her no opportunity to admit her marriage was a mistake, forcing her to live with it and die with it." He closed his eyes. His voice became faint. "If I had only . . ."

The voice stopped. Shanley stared at him. He hurried to find Paula and met her as she was coming through the living room toward the study.

"I was coming to break it up," she said.

"He doesn't look right."

Her smile vanished. She hurried to the bed. He stood in the doorway. When she turned toward him she was smiling again. They walked out into the side yard. Summer clouds had moved across the sun. She sat on the stone wall and looked up at him. "He goes to sleep like that."

"My God, he's sharp."

"Sometimes he goes a little off. Not often. And it makes him very angry when he does. He goes into the past, and becomes confused about who I am and why he's in bed."

"What are you doing for him?"

She shrugged. "Keeping him clean and comfortable and entertained. What else is there to do? Ward Marriner is an excellent doctor. The malignancy is slow and localized and not pain-making. He'll die easily, Sid."

"When?"

"Soon. But I have a very unprofessional opinion about that. It won't be tomorrow or the next day or the day after that. Because he wants to talk to you and listen to you. And to George."

"When does George get here?"

"This evening or tomorrow. Do you mind listening to the old man?"

"Funny question, Paula. I don't mind. It's a very strange feeling. I didn't think I had anybody. Then there's this link, going so damned far back. Way back. For God's sake, *his* father knew Lincoln!"

"Don't you want roots like that?"

"What good do they do me?"

"A sense of belonging, Sid. Small towns are full of all the tangled roots. When your mother was a little girl she played in the yard. She sat on this wall. That was her room up there. She looked out of those windows. When I was eleven years old I fell out of that crab apple tree on the other side of the road and chipped this tooth. See? My best friend lived in that house over there."

He looked at the stones of the wall. "Stop trying to do it," he said. "Stop trying to pull me into all this . . . damned identification. Last night wasn't any lifetime guarantee." He heard the words after he said them, knowing how deeply they could hurt her, and he was aware of her stillness and afraid to look at her. When he did look at her, he saw what effort the smile cost her, saw the tears standing in her eyes, and marveled that she could smile.

"Oh, Sid," she said. "That damned door, with the rusty hinges. I pry it open a little way, trying to let some fresh air in, and then you suddenly get terrified and you slam it shut. And you try to slam it on my hands, don't you?"

"I just want you to understand . . ."

"You don't give me credit for understanding. What am I supposed to be? Some sort of dangerous swamp? Last night was complete in itself. I won't let you spoil it."

He tried to answer her smile. "I'm sorry. I don't want to spoil it."

It had not been anything planned. By Sunday noon he had realized they were getting ahead of schedule. He had stopped at a second rate motel and dickered with the owner-manager and they had been charged a dollar apiece for the use of one unit in which to take showers. She had gone first. When she had come out, in her fresh yellow blouse, she had acted odd in a way he could not identify. He went in, carrying fresh clothing. The little bathroom was humid with steam, mildly pungent with the characteristic scents of her. And on the big misted mirror she had left him a message, written with her finger. A bloated heart, a crooked arrow. P.L. loves S.S. It was both wry game and delicate overture. It was funny, and curiously touching.

Five miles up the road she said primly, "Send a message and nobody answers."

"You see that sort of thing everywhere. Peter Lorre loves Sylvia Sydney. It's one of the true romances of show biz."

"I hate people who think up lines to take themselves off the hook."

"Well, we're running ahead of time. The only possible solution is to find another motel and steam up another mirror and spend the night writing messages to each other."

"Sir! You owe me a message, not a communications center."

"Okay. S.S. loves P.L."

"I'll never believe it until I see it carved into a tree."

"Or painted on a national monument."

She looked at him oddly. "You're getting better, Sid. You were so heavy and kind of reluctant. You were out of practice. Do you know you are actually laughing out loud once in a while?"

"I'm traveling with a very comical woman."

"I swear it, Sid, some day we're going to laugh until we cry. We're going to totter around, weak and gasping, trying to stop and not being able to. And you don't know how good that is going to be for you."

"Climb into the back, woman. You're overdue."

"For what?" she asked with a vast innocence. "Oh! I see what you mean. I should sleep. Yes sir, captain sir. For a moment there I had the idea . . ."

"Nurse!"

With mock haste and fright she clambered lithely over the back of the seat and stretched out. He heard her humming to herself, slightly off key. In a very little while she was sound asleep. The sun moved lower behind them. The big pike rolled through the gentle country.

At two o'clock on Monday morning he was again driving, and they were on a narrow country road just thirty miles from Bolton, moving through the summery moonlight. When he saw the silvered chimney of a burned farmhouse and the slanted roof line of a collapsing barn, he stopped and backed up and turned into the overgrown driveway and, moving slowly picked a way between the saplings and the berry bushes back to a place beyond the barn, out of sight of the road.

When he turned the lights and motor off, the night was all a stillness edged with silver, with a faroff sound of tree toads.

"Is this AAA approved?" Paula asked.

"They're remodeling. Low low summer rates. Cross ventilation in every room."

In a little while they settled themselves for sleep. The night was warm. She had the mattress and made a pillow of the folded blanket and insisted he take the pillow into the front seat. He opened the door on the driver's side to give himself leg room. Their heads were close, but the barrier of the seat back was between them.

"Sid?"

"Yes, Miss Paula."

"Sid, were you doing well in that agency business?"

"Pretty well. We were making the regional distributor happy."

"What were you after?"

"My goal in life? Hell, I don't know. To prove I could swing it, I guess. A little respect. So that anybody looking at me wouldn't know but what I'd been there all along."

"Suppose, Sid, just suppose that all of a sudden you didn't have to run any more. Would you go after the same thing all over again?"

"I guess so." She did not answer. In a little while he said, "No. I wouldn't. I answered too fast. In Jacksonville I was imitating something I'm not. Thelma was part of the imitation too. I proved I could get away with the imitation, and I wouldn't have to prove it again. I don't know what I'd do. I would have to find something. It would have to mean a little bit more, I think." He hesitated. "But it isn't something I have to figure out right now. I'm still running."

"There's always room to run."

"There better be. I'll see the old man. And I'll take off."

Her voice was strange. "What if I don't know what I'm supposed to be, either. What if things don't make any sense to me, the way they've happened."

"Are you asking me something?"

"You don't know how damned many things I'm scared

of. I'm supposed to be a grown up woman. It's like there's a big room and I hide in the corners. Girlish. And I'm twenty-nine. Neither of us are living, are we? Ghosts in the moonlight, and the words don't mean much either."

She stirred, and she was suddenly looking down at him over the back of the seat, a featureless pallor of her face framed by the dark of her hair. She reached and drew her fingertips across his lips. She said in an agonized, secret voice, "Sometimes, right or wrong, don't you have to make something real out of it?"

He caught her arm, then knelt upright to reach her lips. When he ran his hand down the arch of her back she gasped and shuddered.

"Paula. Paula, it doesn't mean that we . . ."

She tugged fiercely at him. "Don't talk. Just please don't talk."

He clambered awkwardly over the back of the seat to be with her. For a little time she was a separate thing, an object for his hands, something he could be aware of as separate as she flexed and jerked and panted under his touch, as he peeled the gunmetal fabric back from the moonlight white bursting of flesh. And then soon he lost his own identity as never before. They became one creature, wise and knowing in its own sweet uses of itself, catching its breath in the slow hesitant ecstasy of union, then tipping and tilting into itself with a long deep sweet pulse of purpose, blended and knowing and growing. A thin voice called him, in a rising joy and plaintive impatience, and he lifted to it and roared his response and went tumbling after, to die very savagely and then very gently, and then with no movement at all in the deep clench of moonlight, adrift in a silence of bug-whine and toad-sound and distant farm dog, their hearts sobering, a deep breath catching from time to time, and the little symbolic offerings of kisses for the cooling flesh, caresses like the last echoes of a great sound that had filled the world.

She rolled her lips into the hollow below his ear, tautened the long softening scissors of her thighs and said, "I love you, I love you, I love you, I love you," said it in a blurred and drunken little voice, all bees in a honey patch, her temples sweaty, her hand patting his shoulder as if in reassurance.

"All hundred percent," he said in half question, turning her, stretching beside her.

"Hundred and ten," she said. "The lady shamelessly willing. You see, it was this damn jiggly mattress." She giggled. "Undermining my virtue for hundreds of miles."

"Never trust a sneak."

In a sudden and resolute tone, she said, "My God, it's valuable to have something so final and true you can joke about it without making it trivial. Something you can't talk to death and you can't remember to death. Something that just *is*, now and forever, the way I always thought I might able to be with someone and never was. If I died yesterday, I'd think it was all a big cheat, and if I die tomorrow, I'll have, right at the end, a funny little smile. Hey! *That's* the smile on the Mona Lisa, Sid darling. I never knew it until now. She's saying we can do anything to her we want, and it doesn't matter a bit, because once she stopped the whole world for a little while. I'm babbling. I don't care. You have to put up with it. I don't have to worry about you, sir. I don't have to ask you how it was for you. I *know* how it was. It was for you as it was for me, because there was only one of us."

"You're a rare thing," he said.

"I've got Indian blood."

"That John Smith was no fool."

He sat up and shook the blanket out and spread it over them. When he lay back, she hitched upward until she could hold his head against her breast. She stroked his cropped wiry hair. She crooned to him, "Now you're not running. This is where you're safe. I love you. This is where you're safe."

It bothered him a little. He wanted to try to tell her that it could never be quite that simple. But the voice and the warmth and the closeness took him down into sleep, his face against a sweet plumpness of velvet, each breath scented with her, with the faint aromatic musks of her, the gentle fragrances of love.

He awoke to early sunlight. It had heated the interior of the wagon, and in their sleep they had pushed the blanket aside. Their clothing lay entangled where they had thrust it away. She lay curled with her back to him, taking up all the narrow mattress, and his hip was lamed where it rested on the hard floor of the wagon. He stroked her awake, and she gave a gasp of surprise, a leap of astonishment. They were sweaty from the imprisoned heat. She was uncertain for a little while, her body awkward, her eyes evasive, but soon she limbered into her wanting, her expression inward and watchful, her responses taking them back to what they had learned so surely. When it had ended, and, in their diminishing, they drifted back into their separate identities, she laced her hands at the nape of his neck, smiled at him, kissed the tip of his nose and said, "Good morning!"

"A lovely morning."

She looked gravely at him. "This time was different. It was as much, but different."

"Yes."

"A little bit of sadness mixed in with this time, Sid. A little bit of despair. Like putting something away to take out later."

"I felt that too."

"You don't have to say it. We'll always feel exactly the same thing in exactly the same way. Not before and not afterward. But during. No, don't leave me yet. Not for a minute. I want to say a funny kind of thanks. What we have, I tried to find it before, Sid. I tried to find it with one man I thought I loved, and I tried to find it with my husband. I've always known I was . . . well, lusty is a good enough word, I guess. And I thought the way to it was through sensation. To have them help me get myself so terribly worked up, that I was practically out of my mind. I've never talked like this to anybody. I would get . . . carried away. I guess I scared poor Jud. But it would all be . . . a self-involved thing. All my attention would be on me. And I would achieve . . . a terrible, grinding, screaming climax where I didn't even know who I was with. But it was only skin deep, sort of. The moment it was over it was over. Without sweetness. And I would feel sort of mealy and sick, and I wanted to roll myself up into a ball and have them go away and not touch me. Can you understand that? But with you, I don't *need* all the little things that take me so far. They're sort of all there to begin with. And all the way through I know it is you. Completely you, like nobody else in the world can ever be for me. Somehow I knew that when I saw the picture of you that Fergasson brought. I knew it way back then. I'm aware of you, and it happens more than skin deep. My God, it happens in every tiniest nerve and muscle, and most of all in my heart, and afterwards there is this aching sweetness and tenderness and holding and loving. Nothing mealy, and nothing sick. So this is a funny kind of thanks, for letting me find out I'm a woman. And right now I have the feeling I'm crying without crying at all. I'm a woman, and I'm your woman. And I would die for you."

"Paula, Paula."

"Hush up! I don't want affirmations you don't want to give. I'm not fishing, my friend. I made my affirmation, and so did you. Now do we stay right here all day and lose twenty or thirty pounds?"

They got out into the tall grass that tickled their calves, dried themselves on the blanket and on the shirt and the blouse discarded the previous day. When she went off behind the bushes, he walked down to the end of the back pasture and found an icy brook at the edge of the woods. He followed it along and found a deep black pool under the shade of a stand of willows. He went back and got her and they went back to the pool with toilet articles and fresh clothing and the improvised towels. He had soap in his toilet kit.

She stripped and tried to lower herself into the black water, holding onto willow roots, yelping at the iciness, gasping and chattering, until he pried her hand loose and shoved her in. She came screaming to the surface, and her long body had a saffron look under the cold water. She swam hard. He floundered in and it took his breath. In a little while they were reasonably able to endure it. They played and laughed and splashed and then, in the shallows on the far side, standing in the yielding mud of the bottom, took turns with the soap.

She rinsed and watched him. "I like your body," she said. "I like the way the muscles are sort of long and flat and they pull tight when you turn and bend. What's that mark on the back of your left thigh, dear?"

"Purple heart. Silly goddamn thing. Night patrol and they heard us and put a flare over us and I sent everybody into holes and then ran like hell and went diving into one myself, rolled over and over and landed in the lap of one of my guys sitting there holding a trench knife. We thought it was very very funny until I passed out on the way back home from loss of blood."

"It makes me feel sick to think of that body I love being where there are sharp things and bullets and blood. I don't feel strange about looking at you. As a nurse I've looked at hundreds of naked men. But I always felt a little strange about looking at their sex. Not shy about it. But as if it was something kind of . . . ludicrous and sort of self-important. But not with you. You look dear to me, and bold and . . . like statues. That must mean something, to have it be so different."

"Maybe it means trust," he said, and waded deep to rinse away the suds.

She looked startled. "That could be it." She waded all the way out and stood on the bank. She said, "I want you to look at me."

"I have been."

"No. Really look. I never wanted to be looked at. It always made me feel sort of . . . impatient and silly for anybody to want to look at me. But I want you to look. I wish it was better for you. If my hips were a little smaller, and my legs weren't so heavy up here."

She stood in a slanting patch of morning sunlight, with the darkness of the woods behind her. She turned slowly, as gravely sweet and remote as a model. Her body had an ivory duskiness, the lines long and firm, breasts round and high and widely set. There was a soft and muscular sweep to the depth of the belly, and a slight hollowness of spine that gave an impudence to the strong buttocks.

"I wouldn't change it, Paula."

"I'm glad."

"You're a lovely woman."

"For you."

They took the blanket out into the edge of the pasture and lay on it, and the grass was flattened under them and tall around them, making a private world in the sunlight. And afterward, as they walked back toward the car, hand in hand, she said, "The first was magic, and the second was sadness and this last time was truth.

What is happening to me? I want to say things and I have the words to say them. That never happened before. I want to disappear into you like a second heart. I never knew that feeling before. I don't have enough gifts for you."

"I'm not worth the ones you have."

"Neither am I," she said. She grinned at him. "That's the new arithmetic, lover. The sum is greater than the total of the parts."

To their enormous astonishment, when they drove out from behind the shelter of the collapsing barn and turned east, it was only twenty minutes before nine. She sat close to him, her hand on his thigh. She hummed her small songs, and her eyes looked smiling even when her lips were not. She pointed out things to him as they neared Bolton. "We had school picnics down there by that stream," she said. "See that big elm tree beyond the picnic tables? That's where I was kissed the very first time. I was twelve. It was a game, and Ormie Gerner was It and he picked me. We had to go around behind the tree, and when we got there he said in a very jittery way we could just stay there a couple of minutes and then go back to the others. I guess he picked me because he thought that would be all right with me. His eyes were all goggly. So I grabbed him and kissed him a good one. I was a very forward child. He told his friends, with embellishments. I got a reputation of being a very hot little item."

"Now I know where to carve those initials."

She pressed her cheek against his shoulder. "I love you for saying things that make me feel good, and now I have to go way over there and sit up straight and look cool, because we're coming into town, right over that bridge, dear."

"You have no family left here, Paula?"

"None here. A married sister in Perth, Australia. Suzanne. And her three boys I've never seen. A cousin out in Montana. Frank. There was nobody left here when I came back to take care of Tom. A town this small is sort of like a big family. But they disapprove of me, sort of. There was the early reputation, you see. And becoming a nurse, and being divorced sort of confirmed it all. And now I'm trying to work on that poor senile old man so he'll leave me his money. They wouldn't give me credit for being a damned good nurse, or for being necessary to that old man. Emotionally necessary as well as medically. Here's the town. Remember it at all?"

"No."

"Keep on this road. See, we have a few summer tourists roaming around this time of year, but we don't let them disturb our deep sleep. We were both in this town at the same time once before, Sid. You were a frightened little boy. I was cooing and sucking my toes. No. There's five years, isn't there? I guess I was curled in the womb, big as a mouse, but I was here when you were here. A foetus looks so ancient and wise. It knows everything. And then, when it is born, it forgets it all and has to learn it all over again. So I probably knew about you and I was all curled up and dreaming about you, and knew just how it would be. That's why it doesn't seem such a surprise now. I'm just learning all over again what I used to know. There's the house and the iron fence, and that's the driveway at the far end of the fence. Turn in there, dear."

Now she sat on the warm stones of the wall and he looked down at her and said, "I'm sorry. I don't want to spoil it."

"You can't," she said. "That's the point I have to make. It wasn't conditional on anything. I want you close enough to touch for the rest of my life. I have to admit that. You know that. But if last night and this morning in the car and in the field was just . . . a way to try to trap you and hold you, then it wouldn't be worth what it was worth. And there will be tonight too, and if you leave tomorrow and I never see you again, I am your woman and I have been your woman, and I wouldn't have it otherwise. Do you understand?"

"I think so."

"You don't have to be suspicious. I'm not a coward, Sid. If I hurt for you all the rest of my life, that's my bargain. I accepted it. Now sit down right here on these old stones and think it over while I go take a look at him."

He sat and waited for her. It confused him that she should feel as she did. It gave him the feeling that he was impersonating someone she wanted. When he tried to be objective about her, he could see her only as a willing victim of her own delusions. But when she was close, and his response was subjective, it did indeed seem like something so special it was worth whatever wounds would come to them. Greater than the sum of its parts.

In a little while she came back across the side yard toward him, her skirt swinging bright in the sun. She stopped in front of him and looked at him with a crooked smile. "Here I am with clothes on, and walking toward you, and suddenly I was so damned shy I couldn't figure out how my arms were supposed to swing, and my knees kept bumping against each other. And by that icy pond I wasn't shy at all. I love you. Darn it, Sid, when I say that you don't have to look so anxious and uncertain, as if you didn't know which fork to use. I'm not trying to make you say it too. Just be smug and relax and be glad to hear it. That's all you have to do. I love you. See? Just look at your woman and listen to her say it. Come on, now. I gave Tom his shot and he went right back to sleep. Jane is fixing lunch for us. I'll show you which will be your room."

"I better get my stuff out of the . . ."

"Davie lugged it up to your room. Come on, dear. I'll show you."

They went up the stairs. He could remember the stairs. They looked smaller to him. Everything looked smaller, more worn and old. And there was a smell of sickness and medicines in the dusty air. She showed him her room. It was in the front west corner. It had been his mother's room. The master bedroom was in the front east corner, across the wide corridor. The room on the west side of the house, separated from hers by a bath, had been fixed up for him. It was a tall, old-fashioned room with massive dark furniture, a corner fireplace, tall narrow windows, a double bed with high carved posts and an ornate walnut headboard.

"The same as last time," he whispered.

"I know. When George arrives, we'll put him right there across the hall from you. The other bath is beyond his room. That door there. We'll share this bath between us. There are two other bedrooms in the back. Jane has one.

Davie sleeps in a downstairs bedroom off the pantry."

"Everybody is pretty far from the old man, aren't they?"

"Not really. Let me show you."

She took him back to her room. There was an inter-com on the table beside her bed. She turned the volume up slightly, and he heard the slow *Doom*-thup, *doom*-thup, *doom*-thup of the sleeping heart of the old man, an eerie sound in the noon silences.

"The microphone is pinned between his sheet and his blanket," she explained. "I don't have to have it this loud. I can go sound asleep, and when there is the slightest change, I find myself going out my bedroom door, putting my robe on and heading for the stairs without even realizing I'm on my feet. Even if it should gradually get faster, that's enough to awaken me."

"It . . . it's kind of terrible."

"Not to me, Sid. It's his heart. It's a tired, courageous old heart, and it kept beating until he could see you. I love him. Part of the way I love you is the way I love him, and the sound of his heart is a closeness. Listen to it a little while. Please." She turned it up further. She sat on the bed. He roamed to the window, listening to the relentless sound. In a little while he knew it would be something he could hear without it bothering him. You had to get over your feeling that each beat would be the last. But what if it was? It was the sound of life, and at ninety-two, he'd had more than his share.

He came back and leaned against the footboard and nodded at her. "I see what you mean. It's all right, isn't it?"

Her eyes were large and her face looked small as she met his gaze. "I have the most shameless and terrible hunger for you," she said. "A devouring thing. You'll be in here with me tonight. I wish it was night now. I can't come to you. I have to stay where I can hear him." She reached and turned it back to a place where he could just hear it. "This bed sags in the middle. Your mother's bed. Your grandfather's heart. Is it too much for you? Is it too strange?"

"No."

"Friday, Saturday, Sunday, Monday. That's all I've had of you. Fifty hours? A little more. Tom courted your grandmother. He visited her for a year. He sat in the parlor with her and they talked together for an hour, every Saturday night. That's only fifty hours, isn't it? But he saw her in church."

"Paula. Please . . ."

"Help me. I don't doubt what I feel, but I have to make things sound better. Nothing is cheap, but it has to sound better. Emotions are going by too fast today. I laugh and cry without making a sound. You have a wife. My divorced husband is coming here Thursday so I can tell him I don't hate him. Some horrible man wants you killed. And I don't fit into my skin the way I did before. The seams have been taken up. Little scratchy things run up and down me. And somehow, what happened last night and this morning are still happening to me. Get out of here. Please get out and go unpack or something. Don't touch me. Just walk out quickly. I'll be all right in a little while. You have to give me a minute."

He went out and closed her door and went to his room. He looked out his windows. He could look diagonally toward the road in front. There were big maples in the front yard, so dense that he saw a few isolated glitterings of blue as a car went by. They had seen him drive through the village. They would know, somehow, about the old man sending Paula Lettinger to bring the grandson home. Texas plates. One of the grandsons. Sidney or George. She had two boys by that Shanley.

The identification in his pocket said he was Sid Wells. But now, for the first time since Jacksonville, he was Sid Shanley. It gave him a little raw quiver of fear. He felt too exposed. But at the same time he felt a strangely sullen defiance. Maybe Paula had stripped some of the caution away, exposing the second layer of pure damned fool.

He unpacked quickly, and then opened the zipper compartment in the back of his suitcase and took out the package wrapped in yellowed plastic, laced with rubber bands. He took it out of the plastic and unwrapped the oily rag. It was a Japanese 25 calibre automatic, showing the pits of old rust spots. When he had been working a lot in Biloxi, he had found it wedged down behind the rear seat upholstery on a trade-in. He had cleaned it, bought ammunition for it, checked it out in an isolated place. At thirty feet he could be reasonably certain of hitting a circle eighteen inches in diameter. The clip was designed for ten, but the spring was so tired, it would push but six up into the chamber. He wiped the grease off and slipped it into the side pocket of his trousers, with a full clip, a load in the chamber, and the simplified safety locked on. It took up little more room than a cigarette case.

It made him feel ridiculous. Hero makes stand in Bolton, armed with deadly weapon. If the two possible decisions were to fight or to run, this little gun fell somewhere in between. It was a symbol of equivocation. This was a ticket to Mitty land, the hero snarl, and pocketa-pocketa while dastards reeled and fell on every side, begging mercy.

Jane Weese served lunch and ate with them on the small glassed-in porch on the east side of the house, on the side opposite the study where Tom Brower lay on his hospital bed. Jane was in her late sixties, a woman with a small head, a large cushiony body, a sweet vague manner, and a large, primitive-looking hearing aid.

"I would never know you were in the house," she said. "Such a quiet little boy I never saw. And toward the end you took to following me. I'd look around and you'd be there, and you'd smile just a little bit. My land, we had a time getting you to smile. Once I reached too quick to pat your head, and you scroonched right down into a little ball with your arms around your head. It made me cry to see a little child like that."

Sid looked over to Paula and saw the tears in her eyes. "Cut it out!" he said.

"I can't help it. You should be a terrible person now, according to all the books."

"Books!" Jane Weese said with a sniff. "I had an aunt crippled up all her life from a stepmother lambasting her with stove wood when she was a little thing, and a sweeter dear person her whole life long you never saw."

"I wouldn't say my childhood did me much good," Sid said.

"Do you mind if I watch you carefully and see what it did to you?" Paula asked.

"Be my guest."

"I'll watch you for a limited time. About forty years."

"What's going on around here?" Jane asked.

"Aren't these little hot rolls delicious?" Paula said. "Jane makes them three times a week."

"Very very good," Sid said.

Paula tilted her head. She got up quickly. "Dr. Marriner. Don't save anything for me, Jane. I've had enough, really." She hurried off. He looked out and saw a portly man getting out of a red sports car in the driveway.

Jane Weese peered amiably at him and said, "That girl has been more like a granddaughter to Tom. In this year —more than a year—that she's been here, she's sat in there jabbering with him for hours on end. When he was up to it." She sighed wistfully. "I was never that kind of company for Tom. They talk about deep things. You know?"

"She's very intelligent."

"You didn't grow up to look like I guessed you would, Sid. You had a sweet little face. The most terrible thing in the world is when you were all alone, you couldn't find your way back to us. I think of that a lot. It would have made all the difference to Tom. Years went by without a laugh out loud in this house, except maybe me and somebody bringing something to the door. Did you have enough to eat?"

"Yes, thank you."

She cleared the table. He looked out and saw Paula talking to the doctor as he got into the car. When the doctor drove away, Sid met Paula at the front door as she came in. She said that Tom wanted to talk to both of them. They went in. He sat on the window seat, Paula on the straight chair beside the foot of the bed.

Tom worked the control buttons and elevated the upper half of his body a few inches. "I find it oddly distasteful to talk melodrama," he said with a withered grin. "As if it were a kind of vulgarity. As I told you before, my boy, I realize that you have come to see me at some risk to your life. Mr. Fergasson has patiently educated me about such risks in our culture, and conquered my disbelief. We had discussed it. The hoodlum empire wishes you dead, for trivial reasons. They did not find you in Houston, so we can say they could not and did not trace you from there to here. And there has been no flaw in our security. Aside from the three of us and Fergasson, no one in Bolton knows of your lurid situation. There is an intrinsic interest in the long lost grandson rushing to the death bed. But no paper will cover it. We have no town newspaper or radio station. Somehow everyone gets to know everything anyway. If you act furtive, my boy, it will excite speculation. I think you should be a very plausible unremarkable fellow from Texas. Nobody in Bolton knows that you ever married, and nobody knows that you ever lived in Florida. So I rather think you would be safe right here indefinitely. Do you agree?"

"It makes sense. If they could have traced me back to you, they would have come looking here two and a half years ago. How do we know they didn't though?"

"Because nobody could come into this town and find out anything without sticking out like a sore thumb. Gossip is this town's industry, hobby and recreation. It always has been."

"Sir, there's one thing I want to get clear. I'm glad I came back. But it wasn't really because I felt some special need to . . . find my roots."

Paula interrupted. "I told him about the money after he said he'd come back with me."

"I was pretty indifferent about coming back, sir. But there was one thing that swayed me. Paula didn't know how this Fergasson located me. You see, it's something I have to know. I understand he's supposed to be very good, but if he could find me, somebody else could find me. I must have left some trail I don't know about. I had to come back to find out how it was done."

"Oh, that's quite interesting, and quite clever. He had the Jacksonville background, and he picked up your trail in Atlanta long after you'd left there, of course. In Jacksonville you wrote the ads for the used car sales. You did the same in Atlanta. He got a lot of those old ads and he went through them and isolated tricks of phrasing and description, and sales gimmicks. He assumed you would still be in the same business, and in a metropolitan area, and be writing used car copy. He went through dozens of newspapers. He found that the ads placed by Trade-Way Motors in Houston had these same devices and turns of phrase. He went to Houston and found that a Sid Wells had composed the ads. He got a look at you, and he knew that it was the same man in the Jacksonville photographs, thinner and more suntanned, without the glasses and with a different hair style. So he took your picture and came back here and reported."

Sid sat with a stunned expression. Then he smiled in a wry and reluctant way and said, "The son of a gun! I never thought of it. But right now I can think of one thing I used first in Jacksonville, and then in Atlanta, and in Biloxi and in Houston. You build traffic at the lot by selling some horrible junkers instead of scrapping them. A one cent sale. You buy the plates. First come, first served. It's an old gimmick. But I used to corn it up by saying they were guaranteed unconditionally for three miles or three hours, whichever came first. A lot of other things like that too. People see the same old ads. You have to say something a little different. And he thought of a thing like that!"

"It's why he's expensive."

"He would never find me the same way again, sir."

"I needed to find you once. Do you mind being here as yourself, my boy, as Sidney Martin Shanley?"

"It feels strange. But I think I like it, for a little while."

"You please me, Sidney. I want the town to know that the old man's grandsons have come back. The wire from George says he will arrive tomorrow."

Sid felt a little tremor of alarm. "Does he expect to find me here?"

Tom Brower looked at him, and suddenly there was no focus or sharpness in those ancient eyes. His eyes and mouth were vague. " 'Licia, don't be scared of the automobile, honey. That loud noise scares horses, but it doesn't scare big girls eleven years old."

Paula went quickly to him and touched his forehead. "Tom?" she said urgently. "Tom?"

He looked up at her. "Who are . . ." The mists went slowly, like a mirror clearing after breath has clouded it. He closed his eyes. When he opened them again, he looked furious. "Damn wanderings," he said. "Senility. Where did I go to, Paula?"

"Alicia was eleven, and afraid of a car."

He smiled. "I was a little bit afraid of it too. An enormous Buick, and sitting in it was like sitting in a tree house. We motored all the way to Syracuse in it, a tremendous feat. Mud and dust and stones and punctures. We started at dawn and got there just before dark. Forty miles. My wife was so exhausted she wept. But what were we saying when I . . . lost touch?"

"I was wondering if George knows I'll be here."

"No mention was made of you."

"Sir, is there any way we can find out if any stranger or strangers come here looking for me?"

"I think setting it up would in itself cause too much talk, my boy. The chance is remote. I have the feeling your luck is good. I think it was bad for a long time, and now it has turned good again. Do you?"

Paula turned and winked owlishly at Sid.

"I feel better than I have any right to feel," Sid said.

"Now I want you to tell me about . . ."

"Later!" Paula said firmly. "He'll be here. You can talk and talk. But not all at once."

"This child is insolent and domineering, Sidney. They put R.N. after their names and become impossible. All right. I'll sleep. One last little crumb of life left, and she wants me to spend it sleeping."

Sid left them. She came out in a few moments. "I have to run down to the village for a few minutes, Sid dear. Walk me out to my car, and then you go and sit in the front room and listen for him. He might wake up, but I don't think he will."

He walked back to the barn with her. Her little English Ford was parked just inside the big doors, heading out. Behind it, in the shadows, was a high square black Chrysler, up on blocks. Davie was clipping the grass at the edge of the drive.

When they went into the barn, he pulled her over to one side, behind the shelter of the edge of the door and kissed her very thoroughly. There was a warm and lingering smell of dusty hay, of animals long gone. She said, when he released her, "You do respond well to your cues."

"A girl says come with me to the barn, it isn't too complicated."

"I'll be gone about fifteen or twenty minutes. When I get back, you can have a nap."

"Is this some compulsion, to put everybody to sleep?"

"You only let me do about one third of the driving. And you have had a few unexpected demands upon you, you know. Let's keep you all fed and rested."

He faked a yawn. "Now that you bring it up."

She laughed and got into her little sand-colored car and went chugging out and up the drive. He watched her out of sight and went back into the house. He looked in at the parchment silence of the old man, and then sat in the living room. He smelled wax and polish and dust. He looked at the worn places in the rug. The high old furniture was in solemn geometry, in silent rural conversation. He heard the slow snick of Davie Wintergreen's shears, and the sleepy chirr of insects in the summer afternoon.

eight

NO SOUND or smell of summer night came into the small suite in an old hotel in Syracuse where George Shanley lay sleeping. There was a clatter and roar of the two air-conditioning units that made the two rooms seem as if they were on some strange laboring conveyance that trundled on through the night.

He had taken a direct jet flight to Idlewild and had flown from there back to Syracuse on Mohawk Airlines. At the Syracuse Airport he had picked up the rental car he had arranged for, a big convertible. It had turned out to be a yellow one. He was not displeased. He had arrived just at dusk.

Before leaving, once he knew his schedule, he had asked Sad Frank Lesca to give him the right name in Syracuse. Frank had looked it up and phoned a man named Casey Stoker. When he was in the hotel, he phoned Stoker's number. Stoker didn't want to be friendly. He sounded bored. Lesca had told him it wasn't a business trip. Stoker sent him to a place called Hill Haven, told him to ask for Sam. He left the rental car and took a cab. It was a four dollar fare. Sam was bored too. These people seemed indifferent to the west coast operation. When he tried to talk about his places, Sam yawned in his face. But the action was good. The tab was on the house, at least for drinks and dinner. Good drinks. Fine steaks. The girl arrived before he had finished his second drink. He'd told Sam something not too young, slim and dark and small, maybe, with a little class, but not so much class she couldn't laugh a little. And for all night.

She went by initials. T.C. Everybody called her Tee-Cee. She had a cute little face and a big pile of dark hair, and a hard narrow little dancer's body. She had a small scar on the bridge of her nose, and gold way back in her mouth when she laughed. She got the money part out of the way real quick, so that it was snapped away into the purse, over and done with so they could forget it. My God, she went through that steak like Sonny Liston. She was a happy kid. She told her troubles and turned them into jokes. She'd been a dancer, gone out to the coast, married a stunt man. After being paid to fall off horses and buildings, he'd fallen off a curb for free, dead drunk, cracking his spine. No insurance. No compensation. They had a three year old kid named Joy. After trying everything else, she'd finally started hustling, got hooked up with a pretty good call circuit. Good protection. The spine was damaged so high up, the husband's health was shaky. And brooding about how she was making a living didn't help him much. When Joy was five, the stunt man died of pneumonia. She quit the business and came back to Syracuse. Joy was nine now. A cute kid. They lived with her mother. TeeCee worked days as a receptionist. She hadn't expected to go back to hustling. But, you know, you get bored. And she ran into an old friend. And then she got lined up with Sam. Really sort of part time. A couple of tricks a week. No slobs and no drunks and no creep routines. Sort of dates.

After the steaks they went back to where the games were. Sam cleared him. He bought a hundred of chips and split with TeeCee. She liked craps. It was easy to see which way they were swinging the game, and he coached her to go with it until she started getting a little too fat, and then he cashed her out with two hundred clear. They were giving him a cold eye, so he put his fifty on the come line and let them take it. He took his fifty back from TeeCee, and without being asked, she cut the two hundred down the middle. He liked that. It showed a nice instinct.

They had vodka stingers out at the bar and taxied back to his hotel. She was a good hard worker, but something about her kept cooling him off. When it was finished off, he turned another light on and rolled her over and looked at what had kept taking his mind off it, a whole spidery mess of narrow little white scars and old welts that striped her narrow back and her hard little butt. It made his stomach feel funny. She started snuffling even before he could ask her about it.

"It was my hus-hus-husband," she said. "He was in that wheel chair I bought him and he was s-still real strong in the arms. And I'd come back from a t-trick and he'd cry and say terrible stinking things to me and say he was going to kill himself. And the only thing I could do that would help him, I'd strip and bite down on a towel or something and get braced good, and he'd whip me bloody. Sometimes I'd pass out. We tried not to make too much noise and wake the kid. Afterwards, he'd put stuff on my back, and I'd help him into bed, and he'd hold me and we'd both cry on account of what had become of us. You see, angel, it was the only thing in the world I could do for him. It was the only way he could feel like a man, the poor son of a bitch. It should have killed him quick when he fell onto that curb, not slow like it did. I can't wear low backs on anything."

"You poor kid," he said. "You poor kid." He turned the light off and held her close and patted her until she was able to have a nice cry.

When she was over it, she said, "Well, he used to knock me around some before he got hurt. You want we should sleep a little now?"

So together they slept in the cold rackety breath of the compressors, his arm across a body as narrow as Liz's had once been, his face nuzzled into the back of the lean striated shoulder, her dark hair spilled, the light of the far lamp golden across them, lost to each other on the far side of their dreams. And should he awaken, she would come back from her sleep to meet her obligation, making for him a sinewy diligence, manufacturing her obligatory cries of acclaim, falsifying her pleasure, while she wondered if her mother would remember to call the man to fix the dishwasher first thing in the morning, wondered if Joy was getting enough out of her dancing class this year, wondered if the blue blouse would be all right for the office if she turned the collar.

In the second floor bedroom on the southwest corner of the old Brower house, in all the sweetness of the country night, in the soft center hollow of the old bed, the lovers lay entwined, murmurous and enchanted, their

hearts slowed for so long that the nostalgia of their caresses was beginning to turn upon a promised edge of
new urgency. The electronic heart thumped, reminding
them of mortality, making love more sweet.

She caught his hand and kissed the palm of it, placed
it carefully back where it had been and said, "Like those
people in the geometry problems, the ones that live on
the surface of the paper, and all they can go is side-
ways. We're that way about time. There's only now."

"Two tenses. Now and soon."

"Don't talk about any other kind of time. We have a
comparative tense though, don't we?" She nuzzled his
throat. "Better. We don't have good, better, best. We
just have better, better, better. We're very limited people,
Sid."

"Caught in a rut."

"You mean in rut. No. That was coarse and vulgar and
wicked. I'm no lady."

"Don't you swoon? Ladies swoon."

"You keep doing that, boyo, and you'll see a swoon,
believe me. Sid?"

"Yes, dear."

"Should I . . . should I try to be a little more passive?"

"Nobody tries to be anything. We just are. No fakes in
the group."

Suddenly she was tense and still. "Listen!" she whispered. "Listen to Tom."

He held his breath to sharpen his hearing.

"Can you hear how it's different?" she asked.

"The heart is the same, but the breathing isn't as
regular."

"That means he's awake. I better go down and see if
he needs anything." She left him. He saw her as a pale
blur, moving. He heard the creak of a floor board and
the slither of fabric as she put her robe on. "Don't move,"
she whispered. "Take a nap. Rest yourself."

He heard the door open and close. In a minute or two
the speaker made a rusty braying sound that made him
jump. He turned it down, and it picked up Tom's voice
perfectly. ". . . materialize like a damned witch."

"All you have to do is think of me and here I am." Her
voice was fainter, but he could hear her clearly.

"I was thinking of you, my dear."

"Can I get you anything?"

"No. You can sit close and hold my hand and listen to me."

"Wisdom out of the night?"

"Even with old eyes and a tiny light, you're beautiful tonight, Paula."

"Flattery will get you somewhere, sir."

"Flushed and tousled and beautiful and in a sweet daze of love, ever since you got back."

"Oh *come* now!"

"Protestations ring strangely false, my dear. When you were both in here this afternoon, your awareness of each other was almost tangible. I should be glad, you know. He is my grandson. I am very fond of you."

"Then be glad."

"I'm a sick old man, but I'm not a foolish old man."

"That's a strange thing to say!"

Sid reached to turn the intercom speaker off, touched the knob, pulled his hand back. If she wanted it off, certainly there was some way she could disconnect it at that end.

"Strange? That is a very guarded young man. That is a very secret and private and controlled and watchful young man."

"I love him, Tom."

"Ah, that solves everything, of course. You lean out of your bower and sprinkle him with rose petals, and a thousand violins play."

"Why are you being so nasty?"

"If he did not have to run, everything would be totally wonderful. Is that what you think? Your love flows one way and mends all. Yes, I'm being nasty. I'm trying to make you think. Sidney is considerably more complex than you care to believe. Is he capable of love? Can he accept love? Can he believe himself worth love? What makes you so certain he is not an emotional cripple, Paula, incapable of love because it was never given to him? If he cannot, in his heart of hearts, truly believe that anyone can love him, then he can not *give* love. He can only imitate."

"What makes you so damned certain of everything?"

"My dear, a man running will try to find a hiding place where he can fulfill his own needs. And this man, this grandson of mine, has not only been hiding from the Florida villain, he has hidden from any significant demand on his abilities or upon his emotions."

"He couldn't afford that!"

"It would be a drive he couldn't avoid, if he was a whole man. Do you know how I know these things, really? Because I was never a whole man. I could not love. I could never put enough value on myself to be able to give love. I drove my daughter away. I substituted pride and coldness and intelligence for a warm heart. And would rather have had the warm heart than anything in the world. You have the warm heart, my dear. You have all the giving. You accept life. He rejects it. As he has been rejected. His mother rejected him by dying. I rejected him by letting him be taken away from here. His father rejected him by not loving him. His brother rejected him. His wife rejected him, brutally. And no matter how hard he tries to believe in your love, in the back of his mind he is preparing himself for you to reject him too."

"No!"

"So he will try to save the hurt by rejecting you first. He'll tell himself it's to keep from hurting you. But hurt you in that way."

"I'm making no claim on him, Tom. None."

"You fool girl, love is the only claim worth adult attention. Your man is lean and decorative. Your man is dramatic. Your man is intelligent. But he is emotionally immature. Incurably. Root him out from behind the wall where he now hides, and he'll dodge behind the next one. And then the next. Your love, unreturned, will not be reinforced, and cannot grow. Now don't argue with me. Talk to him. Question him. Observe him. All I've done is open your eyes. Now you may give me one of those little pills. Thank you, my dear."

"Why should you try to . . ."

"Goodnight, my dear."

The speaker was silent. He turned the volume up until he could hear the sound of the heart and the soft rasp of the breath, at the same volume that she kept it. The door latch made a small sound. There was a hiss of fabric, the thud of a slipper, a tilt of the bed, and she slipped close to him and he took the warm length of her into his arms. But somehow it seemed an imitation of closeness, the ineptness of puppets.

"You heard," she whispered against his throat.

"Yes."

"What does he know about anything?" she whispered fiercely. "What could he possibly know about us?"

"He's a wise man."

She kissed him. She gave him an irritable little shake. "We feel all dull together. What has he done to us?"

"I don't know."

"Where are you? Where have you gone?" He could not answer her. He could not speak. She rolled up onto her elbows and looked down into his face, so close her dark hair tickled his cheek. He put his hands on her and they felt like wooden hands. "Listen to me," she said. "Listen to me and believe me. I love you. You are worth loving. You are worthy of love."

"No," he whispered.

"You are good!"

"I am nothing."

She lay upon his chest and began to cry. He held her and felt the heat of her tears and could not comfort her. He had wooden arms, quartz eyes and a paper heart, and no creature could find comfort in him. Her tears stopped. She sighed, and it was a sound to tear a paper heart. He looked down into himself, into the cave of echoes that was Sidney Shanley and he found something under the floor of the cave. He brushed the sand away with greatest care, and found a membranous thing there, a toughened, leathery, forgotten thing. It pulsed slightly and imperceptibly, and he pulled at it with every effort of his will. Nothing changed for a long time. And then he saw that it had begun to bulge a little more with each pulsation. With jaw and fists clenched and eyes rolled inward, he stretched the leathery carapace until it was so swollen it filled the cave. He held the woman, and called upon God, and took a deep breath, and the dark and hardened thing burst within him. His jaw creaked, and acid spurted into his eyes, and he shifted the woman and rocked his iron face against her breasts and gave a great strangling guffaw of his agony. It was all there at once—a room that smelled sick and her face like candles—she's gone boy—Jane crying as the man knocked her down—and the dazing chunk of fist against his head—Thelma's eyes rolling, and the sound she made —We get fifty bucks a month for giving you board and room, kid, and keeping you busy—rolling in the wet rainy grass in the stink of his own scorched flesh. Child, boy and man, all at once, taking the agonies all at once. He held the woman and sobbed against her breasts and called to her. "Help me! My God, help me!"

She held him and rocked him and murmured, and put her tears with his, and said, "Let it all come, my darling. All of it. All there is."

And after a long time he was still. The emptiness was filled with images and with things learned, but they were tangled, and it would be a long time sorting them, if ever they could be.

His breath caught from time to time, an echo of a sob. He felt drained and weak and strangely placid. She lay beside him, her head pillowed on his shoulder. He touched her brows and her lips with his fingertips. "I love you," he said in a harsh and effortful whisper.

"Yes."

"I can love you. I won't be so good at it. But I do. I can. I can make it good. I can stay with it. I'll want to run."

"I won't let you."

"Whatever happens, you'll be a part of it. Whatever my life is, it will be with you."

"I know."

"And you might regret . . ."

"Hush!" she said. "I am part of you. You are part of me. I'm worth only as much as you are."

He kissed her hair. "That old man," he said.

"Wrong, wrong, wrong."

"Right and wrong."

She stretched luxuriantly against him. "But look at us now. No more dull. All the little nerves reaching. Alive but weary, huh? Let's sleep, my love."

"Yes indeed."

"I love you."

"I love you, Paula."

The goodnight kiss was a caress. And in the process of settling themselves for sleep there were further small caresses. And small excuses for just one more. And another. And it became, in a drowsy way, interrogation and response. A reply and a new question. Another settling, an effort of will, a few innocent slynesses, until finally she laughed softly and turned toward her acceptance of an obviousness and said, "This time sweet and soft and slow and lazy, with time for jokes and wise sayings and protestations of love, and let me be in charge. Like so. And thus. Because you are my man, and I adore you."

nine

THE OLD MAN in the gas station told George Shanley how to find the Brower house. It was two o'clock on Tuesday afternoon. He drove slowly east in the big yellow convertible with the top down, through a tunnel of elm trees, the car radio loud. He wore big dark glasses, and he looked at the tall frame houses of earlier times. A dead place, he thought. A hick operation. The big action is bingo in the church basement.

The Brower place was the one with the iron fence across the front. He turned into the driveway and stopped by the side, near the walk. He turned the car off and got out and stared at the house, feeling disappointed. The yard was in good shape, but the house needed work. It looked as if you could shake it and carved pieces would fall off. The ride up had blown away the last symptoms of mild hangover, but he still felt depressed. Big deal, to inherit the old barn. Who'd buy anything this far from anyplace? If the old bastard had any real money, he wouldn't live like this. He shrugged and divided his minimum expectation by ten. So even ten grand wouldn't be a total loss. It would be worth the trip.

As he took his first slow steps along the walk, a woman came down the porch steps to meet him, wearing a rather formal smile. Dark-haired woman with a strong face, looking a little bit foreign somehow, lean, moving well, built pretty good, looking like class, more than you'd expect from the town and the house, wearing a light green skirt, a white sleeveless blouse, flat heels.

"George Shanley?" she asked.

"That's me."

"I'm Paula Lettinger. We were expecting you a little sooner."

"I couldn't get away as soon as I expected, then I got hung up in Syracuse. A business deal. Two birds with one stone. Did the old guy die?"

She looked startled. "Of course not."

"So a little late doesn't matter. Where do you fit the picture?"

"I'm Mr. Brower's special nurse."

"Off duty?"

"I'm on duty. Mr. Brower is asleep right now. He prefers I don't wear a uniform."

"So what's the routine, honey? He wants to talk to me. So here I am. When can he talk, and how long, and where do I stay?"

"You can stay down at the Inn. It's quite comfortable. Or you can stay here."

George took his dark glasses off. "What's your suggestion, honey?"

She shrugged. "It's up to you. Your brother is staying here in the house."

She saw his curious reaction. His half smile remained fixed. His hand, moving to slip the sun glasses into his shirt pocket, stopped its motion. He seemed to stop breathing. Until that moment she had thought him an absurd caricature of her lover, had seen him as Sidney would be were he made shorter and much heavier and older, half bald, if all the perception and awareness were erased from his face and replaced with a coarse, meaty, animal blankness. But something about his few seconds of an absolute stillness chilled her.

Then the hand moved and the glasses went into the pocket. The smile changed. "Sid the kid, eh? When'd he get in?"

"Early yesterday."

"Lots of time to butter old grandpop, huh?"

"I really don't believe that's why he came here."

"Why should you get sore, baby? You should stick to the pill business. I guess what I'll do, I'll stay here. Okay with you?"

"Mr. Brower said you could stay here or at the Inn."

"So it's okay with him and I guess that's what counts. Do I eat here?"

"If you wish."

"You do the cooking?"

"No."

"Can you show me where I sleep, maybe?"

"Your car is blocking the drive, Mr. Shanley. Suppose you leave your luggage on the walk and put the car out in the back. When you're ready, I'll tell you where your bedroom is."

But when he walked into the front hallway with his suitcase, a heavy old woman was waiting for him. "I'm Mrs. Weese," she said. "You go up the stairs and it's the room right opposite the top of the stairs. Lunch is over, so if you ain't et, you'll have to go into town."

"How do I get some ice?"

"Through that door to the kitchen and I'll give you some if I can spare any."

"Real service around here, mom."

"You get the same as anybody else," she said and turned away.

"Where's my brother?"

"I ain't kept track."

George Shanley had just finished unpacking when Sid rapped on the open door and walked into the bedroom. George straightened and stared at him. "Well, well, well. My little old burr-headed brother. You look great, kid. Just great."

Sid sat on the foot of the bed. "The gathering of the clan. It warms my heart."

"Let's don't crap each other, kid brother. Since I was sixteen I seen you one time, and I haven't exactly missed you."

"So you found other targets for your natural sadistic tendencies."

George leaned against the bureau and stared at him. "Just like in the airport. The big words. You want to be class, Sid? You and me, we came out of the same cellar. You got more school, maybe. What difference does it make? How much did you ever pay for a shirt? This here is an import. Twenny-fi' bucks. I didn't need big words to buy it. Just money. You were a soft, sissy, dreamy little kid, and you're still dreaming. It's my world, kid, not yours."

"What are you so defensive about, George?"

"Stop trying to crap me, kid. What shape is the old man in?"

"Dying."

"How long is it going to take him?"

"Nobody seems to know."

"Not even that snotty nurse? Just who the hell does she think she is?"

"The old man likes her."

"So she's after the loot. It figures. If we didn't show up, she'd make out better. How much loot is there, kid?"

"I don't know."

"You don't seem to know much of anything. Has he decided how to split it up?"

"I don't know that either."

"Anybody else here beside you, me, the old man, the nurse and that fat housekeeper?"

"Just an old man who does the yard work."

"Spooky damn house. You can have it for your share, Sid."

"Thanks a lot."

"When do I get to see the old bastard and do my loving grandson bit?"

"When Miss Lettinger says you can."

"How the hell long do I have to stay here?"

"I don't know."

George stared out the window. "No television. No broads. Do you play gin?"

"No thanks. Have a nice rest."

"Is the old boy upstairs here someplace?"

"No. He's downstairs, in the study off the living room. They had a hospital bed brought in."

"Maybe the night nurse is friendlier."

"There's just the one nurse, George."

George moved over and sat on the bed. "There better be some money in this. I got four kids. Liz and the kids, they're at Tahoe. Liz doesn't like the summer climate in San Diego. It costs to keep them up there. Don't get the idea I'm hurting on the long run basis. It's just a temporary squeeze, on account of a tax audit didn't come out so good. Take the places I've got, I'm grossing over a million a year. But right now would be a good time for some extra money coming in. For God's sake, I didn't

even know I *had* a grandfather. Kid, you look brown
and tough. That your wagon with the Texas plates out by
the barn?"

"Yes."

"What do you do down in Texas, kid? You still in the
car business?"

"Yes," Sid said. He was pleased that his voice was
casual. But he could not trust his face. He walked over
to the window. He looked at the steadiness of his hands
as he lit a cigarette. All the alarms were working. He
went over it carefully, to make certain.

"As long as people like to eat and like to drink and
lay a little bet, I'm going to stay healthy," George said.

"The old man might be worth quite a bit," Sid said.

"You mean it?"

"Well, he might have a lot of land."

"Land can be pretty good," George said eagerly.
"There's a lot of ways to make out pretty good with
land."

"I saw a map with his holdings marked on it. It
looked like a lot of land."

"Where is this map, kid?"

"Down in the barn, in the back. It's on the wall back
there, varnished over."

"Can we go down and take a look at it?"

"I guess so, George. But let's not be too obvious
about it. The old man is still alive. It doesn't look very
good to be counting up the money."

"Sure. I see what you mean."

"Let's go down and go out the side door and wander
around and end up out at the barn."

They went down the stairs. Sid went to the living
room door. Paula was in with the old man, and from the
sound of her voice she was reading to him. He could
hear Jane Weese working in the kitchen. They went out
the side door. The afternoon was slightly overcast. The
big yellow convertible was parked by his station wagon.
Sid looked for Davie Wintergreen and saw the old man,
far off, working in the old orchard on the hillside far
behind the house. He nodded to George to follow him
into the barn. He walked back past Paula's car and Tom's
old sedan, past box stalls to an area used for the storage
of garden tools and supplies. He walked slowly across that

area, hearing George's footsteps close behind him. Sunlight came through small high windows, diffused by dust and cobwebs.

He stopped and turned smoothly, pivoting with an accelerating power, and, keeping his right elbow tight to his side, he drove his fist deeply into the belly-softness of his brother, releasing in that merciless and malignant explosion all the persecutions of his childhood.

George gave a great gagging belch and doubled, his face shiny grey, eyes bulging and lost. He fell to his hands and knees, sucked air with a rasping sound, collapsed onto his side and pulled his knees up. His eyes were closed. He groaned with each exhalation. Sid knelt beside him and emptied his pockets. He pocketed all the money and the keys. He ripped up the licenses and identifications and credit cards. When he put the wallet back into George's pocket, all it contained were pictures of small children and a blonde busty woman with a porcine face.

George stirred, coughed, gagged and pushed himself into a sitting position, his head hanging between his knees. "I think you bust something inside," he mumbled. "I think you busted me up."

"Maybe," Sid said. He looked around the storage area and saw a coil of half inch manila, grey with age, hanging on a nail. He went into the nearest box stall. There was a heavy overhead beam, ten feet off the floor. He tossed the rope over it. Both ends hung down.

George got clumsily to his feet. His face was plaintive. He stood in a huddled way, hugging his belly. "You sprung something, kid."

Sid took his arm and trundled him into the box stall. George saw the rope. "Hey!" he said in a thin voice. "Hey!" He set his heels. He put his hands up and filled his lungs to yell. Sid hit him on the fatty angle of the jaw. The yell became a sigh. He caught George, sat him down like a fat listless child. He tied the rope around his brother's thick neck. Not a slip knot. But snug. The knot was at the nape of the neck. He took the other end of the rope. He took it over to the feed bin, where there was a sturdy cross member.

George shook his head slowly. He looked around. He lifted his hands quickly to his neck. There was a look of horror in his eyes. He took a breath and Sid pulled on the rope. It choked off the yell. George's face began to darken. With surprising agility he scrambled to his feet, whining as he did so. Sid kept the same tension on the line, and then relaxed it slightly and said, "No noise, George. No yelling."

George fumbled at the loop and at the hard knot with thick white fingers. In a gurgling voice he said, "Please! Jesus, Sid, please!"

"Stand tall, Georgie."

George stood very erect. Sid tested the tension very carefully, and lashed the line to the feed bin. George stopped fumbling with the knot. He stood at attention with his chin up. The flesh of his throat bulged slightly over the grey manila.

"You gone out of your mind?" he asked in a small careful voice. "Honest to God, kid, if this is some kind of a gag . . ."

Sid leaned against the bin and folded his arms. "Let's talk about the car business."

"The car business! What's this with the car business?"

"You wanted to know if I was still in the car business."

"Let me loose, kid. Please. What's wrong with that? In Chicago that time, you told me you were going in the car business."

"No, George. I didn't tell you where I was going or what I was going to do. So let's talk about the car business."

"I don't know how I knew!"

Sid put one hand against the rope and pushed. George went up onto his toes. His hands flew up to grab the rope. But he could not ease the pressure. His face darkened, his mouth craned open and his eyes began to bulge. Sid released the pressure. George gasped and coughed and Sid waited until his breathing had quieted.

"How did you know I was in the car business? Think a minute before you answer. You were a mean kid, George. Anything I had, you took it if you could use it, and broke it if you couldn't. I hate you, George. I hate you enough to watch you stand there and strangle. It may happen, whether you tell me or not, but it's the only chance you have. So you better take it. I'll strangle

you, George, and hide you under those tarps, and tonight I'll drag you into a field and bury you deep. I'll
drive that rental to Syracuse and abandon it, and I'll
bury your suitcase with you. I'll tell the old man you
took a look around and decided there wasn't enough
money in the estate to interest you. How long before
anybody will really start looking for you, George? How
did you know I was in the car business? No. Let's give
you a one word answer. Where was I in the car business?"

"I don't know, kid. I just don't know."

Sid put his hand on the rope. "Goodby, George."

"Florida! It was Florida!"

"Who told you?"

"Two and a half years ago. I'll tell you about it. Let
me loose. Please."

"Tell me about it."

"You told your wife you had a brother name of
George in San Diego. Then you got in trouble over the
wife with Jerry Wain. You messed him up. You disappeared. They thought I'd know where you were. Two guys
came out. They asked me nice and then they asked me
rough. But I didn't know a thing. They said you were in
the car business. Please let me loose, Sid."

"Then you got the letter. You're part of the same organization Wain is. What did you do about the letter?"

"I came here. What else?"

"That look of righteous innocence is a little too much."

"I don't know what you mean."

"You'd let them know I might be here, George."

"Kid! You're my brother!"

"And you'd set me on fire for a dollar and a half,
George."

"Why should I tell anybody?"

Sid leaned his weight into the taut line. It took George
up so that his polished shoes tapped lightly at the dusty
boards and he made a slow half circle. He held him
there until his hands fell away from the line. When he
released the tension, George sagged on the line. Sid
pulled his slip knot loose and George tumbled to the
floor. He lay on his back. Sid could see him breathing.
Soon he regained consciousness. With little tugs on the
rope Sid urged him to a sitting position.

"Boardman," George said in a husky whisper.

"What?"

"Claude Boardman. He was big, but now he's out of it. He's got cancer. He knows everybody. He made some calls. Wain still wants you. I had to clear myself. If it looks like I crossed anybody, everything is gone. You understand that?"

"How was it left?"

George fingered his throat. "If you're here, I was to make a call."

"Did you make it yet?"

"When have I had a chance to . . ."

"But you were going to make it?"

"What choice have I got? I got a business to protect. I got a family to protect. What are you to me? Jesus, kid, I can't take a chance on . . ."

The whining voice became a meaningless sound, and his vision blurred, and Sid pulled down on the free end of the rope with all his strength. George came writhing to his feet. Sid closed his eyes and made a harsh sound, and everything in the world was focused down to one raw sensation, the little twitchings and tuggings of the rope. And he knew that in a little while the rope would be still, and he would know a horrid peace . . .

Then something was splatting and thumping against his face, clawing at his hands. He opened his eyes and saw the contorted face of Paula. He released the rope and staggered back and, as he turned away, he saw George fall heavily to the dusty floor, Paula hurrying toward him. Sid walked to the wall and leaned his forehead against the rough wood. He took deep breaths. His knees were trembling. His hands were sweaty. He heard rasping, stentorian breathing.

"I think he'll be all right," she said. Her voice was perfectly flat and calm.

"That's good," Sid said in the same voice.

"Jesus," George groaned.

"Lie still for a little while," Paula said. "Nothing is going to happen to you. You're all right. Lie still, Mr. Shanley."

She came over to Sid. Her face was pale and her lips looked bloodless. "How could you do a thing like that? How could you be capable of that?"

He shook his head. "I don't know. I was trying to bluff him. And then I found out he . . . he promised to let Wain know if I was here."

"But nothing could justify . . . such an ugliness. Nothing."

"I know."

"Do you know what you would have been doing to me?"

"Paula, please. It didn't happen. Thank God it didn't happen."

She stared at him for a long moment, and then went back to George. She talked with George for a few minutes, and then asked Sid to help her get him up to his room. They each took an arm. George shuffled along, his chin on his chest, his hands pressed against his belly. Jane stared at them from the kitchen window, her eyes wide.

He had to rest twice on the stairway. They put him to bed. Paula dressed his raw neck, after phoning Ward Marriner. The doctor arrived twenty minutes later. George obediently gave the fabricated story, that he had tripped and fallen face down on a stake. Marriner prodded him and asked questions. He told Paula what to watch for. He gave George something for pain, and then went down with Paula to look in on Tom.

Sid went into his room and stretched out on his bed. He felt slightly nauseated. He heard the doctor's car leave. Paula tapped at his door. He told her to come in. The sky had darkened. She sat on the edge of his bed, facing him, and took his hand in hers.

"I'm not going to pass judgment," she said. "It shocked me. It scared me. You were somebody I don't even know. But it's over now. I'm telling myself you got it out of your system. It can't happen again."

"I'd like to be sure of that. It scared me too. When I was little I wanted to hurt him. I used to think about it. But he was too big. I'd like to be as certain as you are that it won't happen again."

"I can tell you something that will keep it from happening again."

He frowned at her. "What do you mean?"

"If you can't remember what it would do to me, you could remember what it would do to your child."

"Child!"

She swallowed and smiled wanly. "If wanting has anything to do with it, we've started one."

He sat up and stared at her. "But . . . but I thought . . . you being a nurse and all . . ."

"I'm twenty-nine years old." Her tone was angry. "How much of you could I count on, anyway? Could I stand around waiting for a veil and a cake? And what sterling reputation am I supposed to be protecting anyway? I wanted a child before. But I had an instinct about Jud. I thought I'd better wait a bit. When I knelt in the station wagon and looked down over the seat at you, I'd made the decision. I wasn't going to tell you. If you'd asked me about protection, I would have lied to you. What good is the nice broad pelvic structure, and all this marvelous health? Am I supposed to wear the breasts forever as decoration? My body was waiting for the father, waiting for seed, and when I knew it, when I knew it was you, why should I consider anything else in the world except taking from you the one thing that gives me meaning, no matter what happens? And each time for us, I have been so aware of just that, Sid. Such a pulling and yearning. Such a smugness of absolute certainty. You see, I am quite sure. I don't know why I should be. But I am. In a few weeks some friendly rabbit will confirm it. But already . . . I feel like a vessel. I am carrying. My heart knows it." She began to cry and he gathered her into his arms and pulled her down and held her.

"I had to tell you now," she said. "So you . . . couldn't do any terrible thing. So we'd hold onto every chance we have. I'm greedy, and I'm a coward. If I lose you, I have part of you."

"Don't be defiant about it. I'm glad, Paula. I'm a little scared, but I'm glad."

She sighed. "I guess I cheated you, sort of. By not letting you know. It makes it different. I mean when you know it's for that, and when it happens, it makes it sort of . . . eternal. Tonight, when you know, you'll see how it's different. It's making something. It's making something to love, out of love."

She sighed again and sat up and dug a tissue out of her skirt pocket and blew her nose. She made a wry face at him. "Nothing but emotional turmoil, dear. We'll be old before our time." She sobered. "What about him?" She gestured toward George's room across the hallway.

"The key is on my bureau, by the door. I locked him in. I can't take a chance of his getting to the phone. I went out and took the rotor out of the distributor on that convertible of his. He hasn't any money or keys or credit cards."

"I think it would be very nice if he didn't have any clothes either. Slippers and a robe, maybe. After all, he is an invalid. He's quite a terrible man, isn't he?"

"Mean and weak and greedy. And sad, I guess. He took a lot of thumping. He passed it along to me. You have to realize one thing, Paula. I'm not as safe here as I thought I was. They may wonder why they haven't heard from him. I don't think he's the sort of person anybody is going to trust. I'm being very careful as of right now. I may have to leave in a hurry. I might not have time to make arrangements with you."

"Take me with you."

"You'd leave Tom?"

"No. Of course not. So I have to be able to find you when . . . Tom dies."

"I've never been in Minneapolis. I'll set myself up there. Give me a name, Paula?"

She frowned. "One we can't possibly forget. Let me think. And one I won't mind getting used to. Or having my baby wear. Because if we have to hide, darling, we are going to hide so well we'll never be found. Let me see. That first morning. That lovely cold water. Brook? Brooks. When I was a little girl I had an imaginary hero and I called him Morgan. He was very romantic. Morgan Brooks?"

"On the first of every month mail a letter to Morgan Brooks, care of General Delivery, Minneapolis. Don't mail it from this town. Don't let anyone know about it. After Tom dies, get rid of your car and anything else you can't carry in a big purse. Bring what money you have. Go as roundabout as you can. Buses, trains. Make the trip last a week. When you arrive in Minneapolis, take a room in a small hotel, write your address to me at general delivery, and sit and wait. I'll be established, and

it will be known that my wife is going to join me sooner
or later."

"Say it again."

"Wife."

"Yes. Mrs. Morgan Brooks. And can we get married
really?"

"Of course."

"It's sort of adventurous."

"Not after several years of it, it isn't."

"We'll be safe. I'll keep us safe."

"I . . . I think I can stay at least until your husband,
your ex-husband shows up. I want to be handy when you
go through that."

"I want you to stay, but not for that." She stood up.
"I'm neglecting my patient. We should tell him about
George. Not all of it. But what you found out, at least.
So he'll know why you feel you have to leave."

"I think you're right."

"And Dr. Marriner gave his permission for Tom to talk
to his lawyer in a little while. Randolph Ward. He's bringing out the new will . . ." She looked at her watch.
". . . in about forty minutes."

"Before talking to George?"

"Mr. Fergasson learned quite a lot about George."

ten

IN THE late afternoon, Randolph Ward, Paula Lettinger and Sidney Shanley sat on the enclosed porch on the shady side of the house. Ward had a tall russet pompadour with such a pronounced wave, such glossy health that it made the rest of his face look vague, like a photograph blurred just enough to be unrecognizable. His voice had an equivalent lifelessness. It induced yawns.

"When my father was still alive, he handled personal matters for Mr. Brower. Neither of us ever handled business law for him . . . corporate matters . . . attorneys in Syracuse . . . not enough of the other for a regular retainer . . . but with the will . . . the arrangements with Fergasson . . . not much like the other clients I have . . . he seems weaker, Miss Lettinger."

"What? Yes, I guess he is. He sleeps a great deal lately."

"No pain?"

"Fortunately."

"Because of his age and . . . the will is unusual . . . I want Dr. Marriner to have another doctor look at him . . . both sign a statement . . . question of senility . . ."

"He's not senile!" Paula said.

"Unusual will."

"But who would try to break it?" Paula asked.

"Just in case . . . anybody would think of it. Mr. Brower seems to be having quite a long talk with your brother, Mr. Shanley."

"It's the first time he's seen him," Paula said.

Randolph Ward looked at Sid with an expression of mild query which faded as the unspoken question went unanswered.

Paula went to see if Tom was through talking to

George. She came back and summoned Sid and the attorney to the study. The old man was propped high, papery eyelids closed. He opened his eyes and said, "I've learned no reason to change any part of it, Randolph. Tell them how it will be. Don't, for the love of God, read the damn thing. It's too heavily larded with legalisms. Just tell them."

"Do you wish the other legatees here, sir?"

"If I did, I would request it."

"Yes sir."

Sid looked at George. George sat heavily in his raw silk robe, staring down at the floor. He looked as if the conversation had not gone well.

Randolph Ward cleared his throat. When he spoke his voice had a surprising resonance and precision. "This house and its contents and the acreage on which it stands shall be maintained by the executor, out of funds set aside for that purpose, as a home for Miss Jane Weese and Mr. David Wintergreen so long as either of them shall survive. They shall receive bequests sufficient to provide for their personal needs. Upon the death of the survivor, the house, contents and land shall be turned over to the Incorporated Village of Bolton without restriction as to use or disposition. Miss Lettinger is not mentioned in the document."

"Tell why," Tom Brower said, his voice strong.

"A substantial trust has been established for her, with quarterly payments of income indicated, the first due in a little less than three months. This will continue during her lifetime. Should she die without issue, the principal amount in trust will then be distributed in accordance with a list of charities which include . . ."

"Skip that."

"Should she bear children, the principal amount in trust shall be evenly divided among them when the youngest reaches twenty-one, with Miss Lettinger, if she is surviving at that time, receiving an even share equivalent to that given to the surviving child or children."

"Why?" Paula asked blankly. "Why, Tom?"

He gave her a small, dry smile. "Perhaps I am encouraging fertility. A new way to sire children. Maybe I think you can do better than I did."

"But even if I don't have children, I still . . ."

"You have a chance for freedom of choice in your life. You are a lady, my dear. You now have a chance to live like one."

"But . . ."

"Get to the rest of it, Randolph. I'm very tired."

"There are other small bequests."

"Skip them."

"The balance of the estate will not be divided until the second anniversary of the date of death. If Sidney and George Shanley are both living at that time, the balance of the estate will be divided equally between them. During the two year period they will receive in equal measure the income earned by the monies being held by the executor. Should George Shanley die during this two year interval, or should his death precede the death of the maker of the will, then Sidney Shanley will receive all income and will receive the balance of the estate at the end of the two year period. Should Sidney Shanley predecease the legator, or die during the two year period, all income and the principal amount will be distributed in accordance with a second list of charitable organizations appended to the document."

"What's that?" George demanded. "How does that go?"

"Weren't you listening, George?" the old man said. "In your terms, if Sid dies, you're out. If you die, Sid gets double."

"So what's involved?" George demanded.

Randolph Ward looked inquiringly at Tom Brower. Tom nodded.

"Assuming we're reasonably close on all taxes and estate expenses, and deducting the other bequests, the income during the two year period should be about thirty-seven thousand. Apiece. Annually. The total residual portion of the estate will be approximately one million five."

George jumped to his feet, his expression anguished. "What are you trying to do to me?"

"I'd think it was obvious," the old man said in a barely audible voice. "I'm making you your brother's keeper."

"But what if he gets *me* killed?" George demanded.

"You have a naturally sordid mind, George," Tom Brower said. "Paula, take the loving brothers out of here.

Randolph, I'm ready to sign the damned thing while I still
have the strength. Should Paula be one of the witnesses?"

"I'd rather use the two people from the office I brought
along. And the notary. They're waiting in my car. I'll
go get them now."

Eldon Bertold, alias K. Jones, drove into the village
of Bolton on that warm windy Wednesday, just before
noon. Summer people roamed the street. It was smaller
than he had hoped, a deadend valley town with a single
business block, churches, gas stations, a small park with
a cannon and a defunct fountain, a frame building named
the Bolton Inn, old houses, small yards, iron fences, big
elms.

Yet he felt his cover was entirely suitable to the environment. He had bought a three hundred dollar black
Buick sedan at a used car lot on the truck route in
Utica. He wore a dark shabby suit. He'd brought the old
Hasselblad along, and in a big photography store in
Syracuse he had purchased the other props, while his
cards were being printed. A sturdy, battered tripod,
floods, flash equipment, filters and lenses—and a scarred
old case to keep them in.

He was particularly pleased with the cards. Business
cards. The main imprint was centered—NEW YORK
STATE HISTORICAL COMMISSION. In the bottom
left hand corner was his new name, for this mission. J.
Wells Hefton—Photographic Field Agent. In the right corner he had added a Utica address to match the plates
on the car he had bought there.

He found the ancient, arthritic town clerk in an upstairs office over a drugstore. Once the old man had
convinced himself that Mr. Hefton was not peddling
nostrums or photographs, he consented to phone a woman named Pettingill whom he thought would be of the
most use to Mr. Hefton in his mission. He made a partial
explanation and then turned the phone over to Bertold-
Jones-Hefton who explained it in more detail. Mrs.
Pettingill was the town's unofficial historian, and she
was hard put to conceal her delight.

He had lunch at the Inn, and arrived at Mrs. Pettingill's small frame house at twenty after one. She was a
small, withered, bright-eyed lady in her seventies, with

hair dyed a lustreless black. Her moccasins and summer skirt and blouse would have been more suitable for a Holyoke sophomore. They sat on her front porch while he explained his mission.

"I don't really expect to find very much of interest here, perhaps three or four houses at the most. We are not interested in anything less than a hundred years old, of course."

"Of course, Mr. Hefton."

"You've seen the books we've published on other areas, of course. We've done about a third of the state so far. So you know the format."

"I think I've seen them. Maybe you should refresh my memory."

"The houses are selected for architectural and historical significance. I take more pictures than are used, of course. Generally they use one or two exterior shots and three or four interior shots. And one full page of text regarding the house, descriptive and with historical references. If I find anything usable, you can plan on doing five hundred words on each one."

"You want *me* to write it!"

"Mr. Brildy said you've written up a lot of the local history."

"But not for . . ."

"We have a very limited budget, Mrs. Pettingill. The very most I can promise you is twenty dollars apiece— if I find anything we can use. And it may be several weeks before your check comes through. So I'll understand it if you decide not to . . ."

"Oh, I'd be *glad* to help out. The money isn't important. There are some lovely, historical houses in Bolton, Mr. Hefton."

"If I do find anything usable, with your help, I can assume you'll help me get permission to photograph?"

"Of *course!*"

He smiled at her. "Well, if you're ready, we can take our first little tour, Mrs. Pettingill. You're being very kind."

On the slow tour of the town and the area, she sat beside him with a clip board and pencils, bolt upright, as excited as a child. He stopped whenever she requested it, stared dutifully at the old houses she pointed out, listened to her torrent of description and historical lore. He did not say yes or no to any of her suggestions. She showed him about seventeen houses, and seemed to grow more agitated as he showed no sign of enthusiasm for any of them.

As they drove back toward the center of town he said, "Is that all?"

"All the best ones. Don't . . . you think any of them would do?"

He did not answer until he had parked by the square. "*Any* of them! Mrs. Pettingill, there are five well worth doing."

"Hooray! I mean . . . how nice."

He had memorized the names of the ones which looked and sounded most appropriate. "Write these names down, please. Stockham, Perndell, Kipp, Ormand and Brower. Far more than I expected, to tell the truth." After she had scribbled the names, he said, "Would any of those present any special problems, Mrs. Pettingill?"

"Well . . . the Perndells are sort of odd about such things, and the Kipps won't be back until the day after tomorrow. And old Tom Brower is very very ill. He's dying. Ninety-two years old. And the Stockhams live in such a terrible clutter, you might have problems getting the interior pictures. But . . . I think everything can be managed. After all, it will be a wonderful thing for Bolton. So many old houses just seem to . . . disappear."

"In my experience, if we start at the easiest one, then the rest will fall in line. That would be the Ormand place, I assume?"

"Young Mary Ormand will be delighted. Do we start tomorrow?"

"We could start now, Mrs. Pettingill. The light is perfect for exteriors. And do the interiors tomorrow morning. Perhaps by that time, seeing that they are next door, you might have permission from the people in the Brower house. I wouldn't disturb the old man, of course."

Sid waited on the side porch with increasing nervousness and irritation. Paula seemed to be gone far too long. Suddenly she came around the corner of the house, smiling.

"Who is he?" Sid demanded.

"Relax, darling. He's just a fussy little man who works for the state, going around and taking pictures of historic old houses. See? Here's his card. What took so long was trying to get away from Deborah Pettingill. She's helping him. She's probably the only person in Bolton who knows more about the history of it than Tom does, but she's a truly tiresome old woman. Mr. Hefton really works at his trade, darting about with light meters, moving his tripod here and there, putting gadgets on his camera and taking them off again. He makes little notes all the time and mumbles to himself."

"Does he seem to know what he's doing?"

"I'm not a photographer, but he acts like other photographers I've seen working. Next he wants to do this house, outside and inside. Mrs. Pettingill told him about the staircase. He's all heated up about the staircase and about the mantel in the living room."

"But you can't let him come in here with Tom so sick?"

"I promised to ask Tom. I couldn't get away from Mrs. Pettingill without promising that much. Mr. Hefton said he wouldn't bother Tom at all. It's his choice, I guess. It's his house. And, after all, it might amuse him."

"Are you going to ask him now?"

"Yes. I promised to go back and tell Mr. Hefton. They'll be through over there in a little while. He's staying at the Inn."

"I . . . I want to talk to my grandfather."

She moved a step closer to him and looked at him inquisitively. "You've decided to leave?"

"Yes."

Her mouth seemed to tremble but she did not object. "When?"

"Tomorrow night, probably. It should be tonight, but your ex-husband shows up tomorrow."

"Thank you for wanting to stay, darling. It will be good to . . . have you here."

"When I leave, I'll take George with me. It's a warm season. I'll drop him off, dressed like a bum, without a dime on him, in the wildest country I can find. That will give me all the time I need."

"And I know where to write you and where to find you, and I'll be very very careful, darling." She looked at her watch. "Tom's had a good nap. You can go in when I come out."

When Sid went into the study it was a little after five o'clock. As he sat on the window seat he could see Paula heading next door to give the message to Mrs. Pettingill and Mr. Hefton.

"Paula says you approve of the pictures, sir."

Tom Brower smiled faintly. "It pleases me to think of pictures being taken for their historical importance, with a historic monument like me still in residence. Maybe there will be a footnote to that effect. It never hurts to let the little people pursue their narrow enthusiasms, Sidney, as long as they don't get underfoot. But in deference to your problem brother, I stipulated that all photography of the interior would be limited to the ground floor."

"Tomorrow night I'm taking him away."

"So Paula told me. A reasonable temporary solution."

"That's my specialty. Temporary solutions."

"Do you have to leave so soon?"

"What can I prove by staying? All I can do is increase the risk. Maybe somebody is on his way, to find out if he forgot to follow orders. But there's one strange thing, sir. I don't understand it myself. But I think if it weren't for Paula, I would stay. They have a word for it when a bull picks one place in the ring and decides to do all his fighting right there."

"Querencia."

"That's the word. This is the nearest thing to a home place, I guess. It's a place where I could fight and lose— if it came to that. But . . . for Paula's sake, I can't risk losing. Do I make any sense?"

"Quite a lot, Sidney. But I don't see much of you, do I? Four or five talks."

"I'll say goodby tomorrow, sir."

"And go somewhere and wait with a vulgar impatience for me to die so your woman can join you there, in hiding."

"It won't be quite like that."

"Why not? Perhaps that's the way I'd prefer to think of it. She's one of the rare ones, Sidney. You two are not children, though you seem that to me. Cherish her. I always seemed to love the sick ones. Paula is quick, suicidally honest, forlornly loyal, fastidious and lusty as a brood mare. Use her well, grandson, and she'll reward you."

"On the run?"

"Stay hidden for two years, then buy safety somewhere. It's far better than nothing. I've had years of nothing. I'm an expert in the art of living with nothing."

"After she's seen Heiler and settled that, I'll say goodby to you. I'll leave after dark tomorrow."

"I can last through tomorrow," the old man said. He held out a frail hand. Sid took it, like holding twigs. On a child's impulse he bent and kissed the dry cheek.

"Forgiven?" the old man said with a sour irony.

"Of course."

"You might do at that. You just might. But I was the man for her, really. I was just born sixty years early— a half hiccup in geological time. If she's back now, tell her I dreamed of steak and will settle for chicken broth."

Sid started out, paused in the doorway and turned. "Just for the hell of it, sir, why does George get half?"

"You want it all?"

"That wasn't the question."

"He absorbed half the rejection and half the neglect. And it damaged him more than you."

"Conscience money?"

"All money is conscience money, my boy."

"Especially what you've given Paula."

The old man gave a cackle of pleasure. "Especially that."

eleven

BY NOON on Thursday Mr. Hefton and Mrs. Pettingill arrived at the Brower house, having finished the Ormand house, impressing everyone with his dedication and meticulous care. At Tom Brower's request, Paula brought them to the bedside.

"Just wanted a look at you," Tom said. "Not you, Deborah. The good Lord knows I've seen enough of you in an excessive lifetime."

"Tom Brower!"

"Fifty years ago we ran each other's gamut from A to B, as the critic said, and haven't had a new word or new idea for each other since, and on my deathbed I'm unlikely to give you another chance to bore me. Let me look at this wizard of yours, who, through the magic of a silver nitrate emulsion, optical glass, and some little springs and latches will turn what was a living, breathing house into a set of sterile symbols in a dull book."

"It is our duty," Hefton said, "to record the past for the sake of future generations."

"I suppose," Tom Brower said wearily. "You are talking to the past, you know. And I am told that Mrs. Pettingill here will contribute the text. God knows what she will find to say about this house, but she has always had a febrile imagination."

"Tom!"

"Plus the blessed and mystic ability to take herself seriously, even as you, Mr. Hefton. And me. And Miss Lettinger. All of us made endurable to ourselves by that philosophical myopia which blinds us to our meager worth. I regret I won't be here to examine your book, Mr. Hefton. There are so few amusing things left in the world."

"The New York State Historical Commission believes that . . ."

"Excuse me, Mr. Hefton, but you may now go putter and click at will. I am a rude old man, and it has been many years since I gave a damn what any commission, committee, association or foundation believes in. One man is a significant entity. A partnership halves that value. Three or more men, working together, diminish themselves to zero. Team effort is the stagnation of the race. Thank you for giving me a look at you."

"I must say . . ."

"Run along with the nice man, Deborah. We can all guess what you must say, so there is no need to say it."

When they were alone Tom Brower gave Paula a rather shamefaced smile.

"You *were* rude, you know," she said.

"It sluices out the glands, my dear, relieves tensions. And one cannot leave any lasting mark on such dim little people. Did I hear him bringing equipment in?"

"Quite a lot of lights and things. Mrs. Pettingill helped him."

"Speaking of tensions, you have more than your share today."

"How not?"

"When do you expect him?"

"I think about two o'clock would be right."

"Where are you going to talk to him?"

"On the porch, I think."

"What are you going to say?"

"I'm going to tell him I'm sorry. I'm going to wish him luck."

"What if that isn't enough? What if he gets difficult?"

"Sid will be behind the door to the back hallway. He can hear everything from there."

"How is George today?"

"Surly but docile. He plays solitaire, one hand right after the other. He has a little radio, and he plays it all the time."

"Locked in?"

"Sid thinks it's better that way."

"Sidney is a cautious man."

"George was . . . willing to betray his own brother, Tom."

"Why the troubled expression? Do you want me to say something significant about all men being brothers? Or condemn George? Or sympathize with Sidney, or with you? I betrayed my daughter."

"But that was . . ."

"Less honest than what George was willing to do. For God's sake, stop fumbling with that needle and give me the shot and get out of here. Your sad, anguished face is giving me the pip."

"Don't you have any damned heart left?"

He smiled at her. "Excuse me, my dear. Some days the mere act of dying seems to depress me. It takes too long."

"I'm sorry, Tom."

"You are quick with the needle when you keep your mind on it. If I should forget to tell you, keep absolutely nothing in reserve with that young man. Love him totally, Paula. Totally, obviously, plausibly—and eventually he may come to believe it."

Bertold-Jones-Hefton had given the old house careful study while taking the exterior shots. Yet he faked no part of his procedure. He used slow, fine-grained film, tripod, wide angle lens, a light red filter, and composed each shot carefully. Now that he was inside the house he realized the front windows of the dining room afforded his best opportunity. One, in particular, had maximum screening by the outside shrubbery. After a full hour of work on the living room and the staircase, he carried his floods into the dining room and set them up, telling Mrs. Pettingill that the detail of the paneling was worth recording. She was in complete agreement. After he had a chance to examine the window and plan his moves, he sent her out to his car to search for a non-existent photo-flood bulb and bring it to him.

The moment she left the room he opened the case and took out the little plastic squirt-bottle of graphite, the small screwdriver and the small pair of nippers. Moving with a practiced economy of motion, he slid the window up, squirted graphite in both sides of the frame, then slid it down and up and down again, satisfied with the new silence of it. He nipped the hook of the outside screen until but a tiny thread of metal held it in place. With the window closed, he unscrewed the two wood screws which held the old-fashioned window latch in place. He nipped the heads off the screws and saw Mrs. Pettingill walking toward the front door. He put the latch and screw heads back in place and dropped the severed threaded portions into his pocket, put the tools and graphite back into his case and was studying his ground glass screen as she walked in to tell him she couldn't find it anywhere in the car.

The window satisfied him. It looked locked and secure. But the smallest tug on the screen would snap the remaining thread of metal. And when the lower sash was raised it would go up silently, lifting both portions of the brass latch with it. He was satisfied that the rest of the job would go just as well, that death would look natural enough, and the doctored window would be discovered long after any routine investigation had been completed.

As he was taking his sixth careful photograph of the carved paneling, he heard Mrs. Pettingill say, "Why you must be the young one! Sidney, isn't it? I saw you once in this very house when you were a little boy! I'm Deborah Pettingill. I guess you've heard your grandfather mention me."

The man murmured something. Bertold-Jones-Hefton turned casually and looked toward the man. But he was beyond the floodlight, in the doorway, a vague figure. He turned and left.

As Hefton changed his setup to get the final wall, he said casually, "Does that man live here too?"

"Oh, no. Don't you remember? I told you about the two of them, Sidney and George. The grandsons. It took Tom a long time to have them found. It's wonderful they could get here before he passed on. Tom disowned his own daughter, his only child. Those are her two children. They say Tom is leaving everything to them."

"Very fortunate for them."

"But Paula is getting a very nice trust fund. Very nice."

"That's the nurse?"

"Paula Lettinger. She comes from here, you know. Odd girl. Hard to understand. She made a very bad marriage, and it was annulled and her husband has been in prison for five years, and he's coming here to see her today, I think. At least, that's what they say."

"I wish I could do some of the rooms upstairs."

"So do I, but Tom said no."

"I guess they're all occupied."

"Oh, no! This house is larger than it looks. Jane Weese is in the back and there's two more empty servant's rooms. And even with Paula and the two grandsons up there, there would still be three empty rooms at least. I know Paula has the front corner room on the west. And I don't imagine Jane would put either grandson in the master bedroom. To her way of thinking it would still be Tom's room, even though he'll probably never see the inside of it again, poor soul. But they'd be toward the front of the house, handiest to the staircase. Jane likes to save steps, at her age."

"The master bedroom is the front east corner?"

"Right above this room, yes."

"I think we're through here, Mrs. Pettingill."

"It's such a lovely old house."

"Isn't it."

"What will we do next?"

"The exteriors of the Perndell house, if that's agreeable to you."

As they were driving away, Mrs. Pettingill said, "Slow down!"

"What is it?"

"That's him, I bet!"

"Who?"

"The husband. Weiler or Heiler or something. She met him in New York. He must have come on the bus, because that's Del Barney driving him out here, and Del does taxi work when he's finished on the mail route."

Hefton looked back and saw a tall man in a wrinkled grey suit walking from a green car toward the front door of the house.

Judson Heiler sat on the glassed porch with the woman he had been married to. He was nearly forty. He had a big unlined face, mild blue eyes. He shook his head slowly. "I can't get over it, Paula sweetie. My God, you look lush."

"What are you going to do?"

"That's a good question. That's a very good question. I gave them their five years."

"Did it have to be five? Did it have to be the whole thing?"

"Honey, it's dull in there. My God, it's dull. So every once in a while you have to jack it up a little. They didn't think it was very funny. And then I had a habit they didn't like. When anybody shoved me, I shoved back. I don't like to be touched. You know that. I get annoyed."

"But what are you going to do?"

"You keep saying that, don't you? I have fifty-five dollars and an unlimited future. What I do is up to you, I guess."

"I don't understand you, Jud."

"Sweetie, what we got here is a case of moral obligation. I did a lot of thinking. You know what our trouble was? You were trying to make me into somebody else. And I dragged my feet. I talked to the psychologist up there. I fought you, baby. I fought you with bottles and broads. With a bottle I could turn myself into somebody else without any help from you. And become somebody else in the snow job I'd give a woman. I'd lay in their arms and talk about you. I'd talk about my big old wife, and I'd wait for you to punish me. But you'd just go around with your face all pinched up, looking noble and decent and full of suffering, and there I was with all that guilt, and no place to put it."

"I'm glad you understand. It took me a long time to understand too, Jud."

"So here I am at long last, baby, saying you win."

"I don't understand."

He shook his head. "Sure you do. I give up. Here is the raw material, and I become just what you want me to be. No dragging the feet. No guilt. If there's no guilt I won't have to go looking for punishment by writing bad paper."

"Jud, you have everything wrong! I wrote to you to come see me so I could tell you that . . . I wish you well. There's no hard feelings. That's all, Jud. I want you to have every happiness."

He smiled and frowned simultaneously. "Sweetie, you are not tracking. You can't pull a man down and win your battle and then not pick up the reward. I'm here, baby. I'm with you. You own me. You bought me the hard way. We go on from here."

"No, Jud. No."

He stood up, smiling. "You certainly look gorgeous. Honey, if you want to fight it a little, to save face, that's okay too. I'll be around. I'll be around every day. And I'll howl outside your window at night. I'll sing our song. I'm loyal as a dog. I'm the sweet husband for you. And I know you, Paula. You *always* live up to your obligations. And I'm it. Sweetie, you should have gotten married if you wanted to be out of the target area. See you around. I can find my way out."

As soon as Heiler left, Sid came out onto the porch. Paula ran to him to be held. She was trying to laugh but she couldn't. "Did you hear him? Did you hear that? Did you ever hear such a crazy thing in your life?"

"He means it."

"But I don't want him back! It's insane."

"What if I hadn't come into your life?"

"Well . . . I guess I would try to help him. I guess it was partly my fault. But I'd never take him back."

"He's going to be bothering you after I've gone."

"I can handle it. Really. I can make him understand."

"Can you? You seem a little shaken up."

"I'm all right. Really. Only . . . don't leave just this minute."

He kissed her. "I'm going to leave a little before dawn."

She hugged him with all her strength. "Out of my bed and off into the cruel cold world," she whispered. "Oh, how I'll miss you!"

"I'll take George along with me. I'll put the rotor back in his car and give you the keys. The pink sheet from the rental outfit is in the glove compartment. Hire some kid to drive it to Syracuse and turn it in and pay for it. They don't care who brings it back as long as they get their money and their car."

"Does George know?"

"It's going to come as a surprise to him."

She pressed close to him. "Tonight I'm going to give you a lasting goodby, Sid. It will last until I see you again, believe me." She backed away, flushing. "Now I've got to go tell Tom how Jud acted. He's in there itching to know."

"I'll come with you. I want to hear him laugh. He has a very dirty laugh."

"Sir, you are speaking of my benefactor."

"I keep forgetting you're a rich nurse."

"Not rich," she said with a smug and knowing smile. "Just terribly comfortable."

Bertold-Jones-Hefton spent the last few minutes in his room at the Bolton Inn smearing all the areas where he could have left fingerprints. He coated the pads of his fingers with transparent model cement. He left the room at midnight. He paid his bill to a sleepy desk clerk and left an envelope at the desk for Mrs. Pettingill, explaining that he had been called away to do some retakes in the Buffalo area and would be back in several weeks to complete the job in Bolton, assuring her he would get in touch with her at that time, and thanking her for her cooperation. He had typed the note on the old machine available for guest use, typed his most recent name, scrawled a single backhand initial. When he had first arrived, pleading an arthritic stiffness from the long drive, he had talked the clerk into signing him in. So there was only one disguised signature in existence, and that was on the vehicle registration for the used Buick, and if all went well, it was unlikely that would be traced. Even if it was, he did not see how it could do them much good.

He drove away from the center of the village, wearing a dark long-sleeved sports shirt, dark slacks. The village slept. He turned the engine and lights off, drifted for the final hundred yards and put the car into the overgrown driveway of an abandoned house. From there he took the route across the fields behind the houses, the route he had scouted while taking the exterior shots of the two neighboring houses. He circled the Brower house in absolute stealth, gratified to note that the few street lamps were as feeble as he had assumed they would be. Aside from a night light in the room of the dying man, the house was in darkness.

He went to the prepared window, put the tiny pry bar between sill and screen and levered it gently. The hook parted with an almost inaudible ping. But he listened to the silence for a time, his eyes closed, before lifting the screen off the top hooks and setting it aside.

The prepared window made no sound as he eased it up. He went up and over the sill with a single lithe muscular silent movement, then crouched inside, knuckles braced against the hardwood floor, head tilted, listening. Soon he stood up, slid the window back down slowly and silently, by touch fitting the shortened screws back into the holes. He drifted to the front hallway and to the front door and listened again. He unlocked the front door. The latch made a single brisk clack, and once again he waited. He opened it eighteen inches, slid through, pushed the screen open. The spring made a soft pinging sound. He closed the screen door carefully, went back to the window, hooked the screen in place, shoved the bottom of it in against the sill, went silently back and re-entered the house by way of the front door. He left the front door barely ajar. After a long pause, he started up the stairs, taking two stairs with each slow step, planting his feet close to the wall where they were less likely to creak.

Paula knew both her men were asleep. She could hear the familiar cadences of the sleep of the old man over the bedside monitor. And Sidney's breathing had deepened, and his arm felt leaden where it rested across her bare waist. Sleep well, she thought. Be safe. Stay safe for me. You are my dear one. You are my life.

The old man was in a dream. He knew it was a dream and he knew he did not like it. He had been walking down some sort of a tunnel, and he had noticed that it was getting narrower and lower. Now he was forced to crawl on his hands and knees and soon there was not enough room for that, and he had to wiggle along on his belly. But the side walls had begun to brush his shoulders and he knew that if it got any narrower he would be stuck there until this miserable dream ended.

George, in his dream, was heatedly, irritably, impatiently undressing Mitz, eager to get down to that tawny sturdy exotic flesh, but under each garment there was another garment, and as the pile of clothing grew around them, she kept giggling, writhing, making it more difficult.

Jud Heiler sat under a maple tree in the front yard of the dark house across from the Brower house. He shook the bottle and estimated there was a couple of inches left. Did the whole tour, he thought. No hold on me.

Drink if I feel like it. No damn parolee. He took two burning swallows, gagged, and set the bottle aside with exaggerated care.

Over there my true love sleeps. A great big gorgeous broad, full of competence. All ready for taking care. That was the penalty for being strong. God gives you a weak one to take care of. One little divorce can't interfere with an essentially symbiotic relationship, ducks.

He beamed across at the old house. He thought of her in there all sweet in her bed, and he had a little pang of uncertainty. At first it had been fine, and then it hadn't been so good, and then he had begun to dread it, and finally it just stopped happening. The psychologist was very understanding. Guilt and anxiety. Psychological impotence.

With no guilt any more and no anxiety any more, it would probably be just as good as in the beginning. If she'd take it a little bit easy until he got used to it. Hell of a vital woman.

He peered into the darkness, thinking he saw some sort of vague and shadowy movement near the front door. He watched, but he didn't see anything else.

He wondered what he should do. There was a lot of time. The thing to do was serenade her. Make her aware of old Judson out here in the night, singing his heart out. But what was *their* song? Couldn't remember it. Bad form. Women like the little sweet stink of nostalgia.

He lurched to his feet, accidentally kicked the bottle over, dived for it and saved but about one inch in the bottom. Very wasteful. Very careless. Drink it to save it, lad. He finished it and set the bottle down very neatly and carefully. He brushed his knees off, deciding that in the absence of a special song, any good old song would do. He had the feeling that he was in fine voice.

"Dum dum dum dum. Do re mi fa so." Lot of resonance in the old pipes.

When the world steadied down a little, he would march over into the yard and try a nice melodic mating call.

In the upper hallway Bertold-Jones-Hefton had oriented himself with the calculated risk of a single sweep of the needle beam of his penlight. So the target for tonight would be behind the door on the left or the door on the right. Eenie, meenie, miney, moe.

He put his hand on the knob and turned it a fraction of an inch at a time. When he had turned it all the way he pushed and it opened slightly. He listened at the opening and heard no sound of breathing inside. He pulled it shut and released the knob as slowly and cautiously as he had turned it.

He tried the opposite door and found it locked. This made sense to him. The target was a cautious man who knew there was a contract out on him and had nevertheless stayed alive for over two and a half years. He risked a single oblique flash of the tiny light. It was an old-fashioned keyhole. He had come prepared to cope with locks. If the key was in the lock, on the inside, he had a pair of needle-nose pliers, exceptionally thin, with which he could reach in and grasp the key and turn it as readily as it could be turned from the inside. He probed and found the key was not in the lock. His set of master keys and skeleton keys were tape-wrapped to reduce jingle. He found the one he wanted by touch alone, inserted it into the lock, and tested it gently. He felt the tumbler begin to move and exerted a gentle pressure. When he was past the midway point the bolt snapped over with a dismayingly loud sound, bringing his heart up into the base of his throat. After several seconds he put his ear against the door panel, and when he heard the rhythmic rasping snore inside the room, he was able to breathe again.

He took three long minutes to open the door, enter the room and close it again. The room was pitch dark, and he could not risk a light. He went down onto his hands and knees and began to work his way toward the bed, reaching a cautious hand in front of him after every forward movement. The snoring was louder. He skirted a chair and touched what he decided was the foot of the bed. He worked his way along it. When he reached the head of the bed, he straightened up, still on his knees, to make certain from the sounds that there was but one person in the bed. After he had squeezed his eyes tightly shut many times and opened them wide, he was able to achieve just enough night vision to show him the vague outline of the sleeper. He was on his back, his left side toward Bertold.

When Bertold was certain, he took the silent weapon out of his shirt. It was based on that homely tool of the Japanese assassin—a sharpened length of umbrella rib. But this was a six inch length of slim, superb steel set into a practical, homemade wooden handle, narrower than an umbrella rib, sharp enough to make a minute and almost painless puncture in the skin, but blunted enough to slip between ribs rather than catch in the bone itself.

He edged closer, held the handle in his right hand, laid the tip of the blade along the index finger of his left hand, slowly reached out until his finger touched the rib cage. As soon as the fingertip settled into the indentation between ribs, and the sleeper stirred, the right hand slid the blade into the heart, then jabbed with several short swift strokes, turning the handle slightly each time, inflicting a maximum damage.

There was a wheezing intake of breath, a hard gasp, a spasm, another spasm, and then a long rattling sigh. Bertold held his breath and he could hear no sound in the room. He wiped the invisible blade on a scrap of tissue, folded the stain inward and put the tissue back in his pocket, the blade back into his shirt. He stood up and turned his penlight on the dead face. He turned the light off, stood in the darkness and shut his jaw so hard his ears rang. All this delicate, perfect, professional effort to kill the wrong man, to give him a plausible, unremarkable, fatal heart attack in the middle of the night. Probably the brother. What was his name? George. No loss to anybody, particularly, but it complicated the hell out of this job. Two identical deaths were out. If they weren't identical, maybe it could be worked. He felt the indignation of the master craftsman who sees a superb effort wasted. He turned the light on again and, aware of his responsibility to his trade, wiped the single drop of blood from the rib cage. The orifice he had made was almost invisible, the flesh puckering, closing the opening.

He told himself that he could not have risked the light. He told himself that it was a perfectly understandable accident. But he knew that he could not rationalize this mess. He had been too anxious to believe that it would be this easy. He had not felt right about this one. He had thought himself calm, but in actuality the fear had been so great he had not taken the elemental precaution of being certain of his man. From that horrible old woman's jabbering, he had learned that Sidney Shanley would be either in this room or the one across the hall. That meant George had to be in the other one. And he had found one empty room, and the door locked on the other one. He had thought it Sidney Shanley because he wanted so desperately for it to be Sidney. This, he decided, had better be the last one. And this one was bitched. The next move was to get out of this room and out of the house and out of this stinking village, to a safe and quiet place where he could think it over and decide what to do next. He moved through darkness out into the hallway, closed the door and locked it again. He stood in the silence, hearing a meaningless creak of the frame of the old house. He moved silently toward the stairs.

The abrupt change of the sound of the old man's breathing brought her up out of her dream, her heart in her throat. It was a sound she had never heard before, a laboring gasp. She slipped out of her lover's arms. He made a sleepy sound. She stepped into her slippers, snatched her robe and shouldered into it on the way to the bedroom door. She pulled the door open and closed it quietly and ran fleetly toward the top of the stairs, and ran headlong into one of the feral night things, one of the things out of the dreams of terror. She made a whimper as she was caught and turned, and a hardness clamped her throat.

It frightened Bertold so badly, he nearly yelled in terror, but in the first instant he knew he grappled with the silks and warmths and fragrances of a woman. His strong hands went instantly to the lock that would bring a hard pressure against the carotid artery, starve the brain of blood and make her faint instantly. But he was so agitated, he did not get it exactly right. She was a strong woman, made stronger by panic, and he tried to shift the pressure to the proper place. Inadvertently he tried to overcome with strength his momentary awkwardness, and suddenly he felt the larynx go, crushing beneath his fingers with an odd brisk papery feel under the smooth heated flesh of her throat. He felt an overwhelming despair. He lowered her to the carpeting at the head of the stairs, on her back. She was making a horrid little clucking, squawking sound as she fought for air. He put his hand over her mouth. She brought her hands up and held onto his arm, firmly, as though she held the arm of someone trying to help her. She was very strong. She was trying so hard to live. Her lungs spasmed, fighting the obstacle. Then, in her extremity, she began to arch her body like a bow, lifting her hips, letting them thud back. He pressed his hand against the knotted muscles of her belly to hold her flat, and in soundless appeal, his lips moving, he said, "Die! For the love of God, die!"

And then she settled, and softened and was gone. He sat on his heels there for a moment, dripping with sweat.

Suddenly, from outside the front door came a great brassy baritone voice, singing off-key with great drunken confidence. "Gone are the days when our hearts were young and gay! Dum dum dee dum. From the cott-tton fields a-wayyyyyy."

Bertold forgot his tentative idea of leaving the woman crumpled at the foot of the stairs. He sprang to his feet. Every last fragment of composure was gone. He went racing and stumbling down the stairs, whimpering to himself. He burst out through the front door, ran into the hedge and fell and scrambled up.

"Hey!" the singer yelled. "Hey! Hey, wait!"

Bertold raced for his car, the singer lumbering along behind him rousing the quiet neighborhood with his yells. He tumbled into his car and started it and went roaring down through the sleeping village and off into the night.

twelve

AT THREE O'CLOCK in the morning, Doctor Ward Marriner came away from the old man's bedside. He spoke to the woman he had been able to find to stay with the old man. She was a big starched woman, a practical nurse. He told her to watch for any change, and phone him. There was only one change he could reasonably expect.

He went wearily into the hallway. A voice spoke from the shadows at the foot of the stairs, startling him. "How is the old man?"

Marriner recognized Captain Lemon of the Bureau of Criminal Investigation of the State Police, a drab, quiet and earnest little man.

"Dying," Marriner answered. "Where's the rest of your gang?"

"They're finished here, for now. I stayed to ask you a couple of things, if it's okay with you. Thanks for the fast autopsy report."

"Fast and not exactly legal, you realize."

"I'll cover you every way I can, like I said, Doctor. I want to know this. Suppose he didn't kill the nurse up there in the hall. Suppose that drunk didn't see him run out of the house. And tomorrow morning there's a rush call for you to come and look at that George Shanley. What would you have called it?"

"Heart. Massive coronary occlusion."

"But those other things happened, and we did find the scratches that showed the door had been unlocked and relocked from the hall, so we know he was killed with an ice pick."

"I didn't say that, Captain. I said something *like* an ice pick. Possibly a little more flexible."

"Anyway, if it hadn't been for the nurse and the drunken songbird, it would have been very neat and professional. But the reasons bother me. I couldn't get much out of the brother. He was like a crazy man. George was apparently some sort of small time hoodlum from San Diego."

"Something like that."

"And the younger brother, Sid, he was in the nurse's bed. Doctor, what the *hell* goes on around here?"

"A lot of bad luck, Captain. Quite a lot of bad luck, I think. That poor son of a gun heard the commotion and the singing and came out and fell right over Paula's body. Captain, I loved that girl. Not the way it sounds. As a friend. As a good friend, both to me and to Tom Brower. A lot of woman, Captain, in a lot of ways. I'm going to look in on Sid on my way home. See if I can bring him back here and give him a pill and put him to bed. Staying with her like that, he's tearing himself apart." He sighed and shook his head. "Sam Gates doesn't get ten bodies a year. Tonight he gets two. And one to go. Captain, if you want to know what the hell went on around here tonight, I think you better get that fake photographer and ask him."

"Hefton. John Doe," Lemon said quietly. "A professional, until things started to go wrong. The kid at the Inn took the license number when he checked in. We made the description of man and car sooner than we had any right to expect. It was a break."

"Will you get him?"

Lemon stood up and stretched. "The longer he lasts, the worse it looks. Maybe he had another car stashed. I hope we get him. I'd like a little chat. I would dearly love a little chat with that savage little con man."

At that same moment, Bertold was being picked up at mile marker fifty-one on the Thruway. He had plausible explanations for the trooper, but they were wasted because the trooper knew absolutely nothing beyond his orders to pick up the described car and driver. So Bertold knew he would be held and he knew how wrong it was going to go, and deplored his own failure to get rid of the keys and the little cutting pliers which could be matched to the severed windowscreen hook. And with a complete astonishment at his own mental lapses, he remembered the bloodied bit of tissue in the pocket of his trousers, the tissue he had used to wipe the slender weapon.

During the hours of driving, holding the car exactly at the posted speed, he had known that he should revise plans, abandon the car, concentrate on the specifics. But when he would try to focus his mind, he would feel the woman's hands holding his arm, feel the warm straining lift of her body, hear the horrid clucking. So he would hum and sing to cover the clucking noise and drive on.

Now he could not accept what was happening to him. All the explanations—even if anyone would listen—were obsolete.

So he faked a stumble, brought the trooper down with a judo chop, and sprinted toward the high wire fence fifty yards beyond the shoulder, knowing as he ran that he was in a blind panic, and should have paused long enough to kick the man in the head.

As he jumped and grasped the fence, the thirty-eight caliber slug pierced the left buttock, ripped through the groin and shredded the left femoral artery. He lay on his back on the dry grass and looked at fading stars and felt as if the world was falling away from him. The trooper put the flashlight on his face just in time to see the last fragment of comprehension in the eyes as the fugitive bled to death.

When old Sam Gates opened the door to Doctor Marriner, he said in a nervous whisper, "Doc, for gosh sakes, can you get him out of there? It ain't right. There's things I should get started on, Doc. I tried to get him out of there and he didn't even . . ."

"Shut up, Sam," Marriner said wearily. "Just please shut up."

The shadows were harsh in the small back room. There was a bright bare bulb in a wall fixture. The body was on the grooved slab, covered with coarse sheeting. Under the molding of the sheet it was the body of woman, eternal. Shanley sat on a low stool, close to the slab, the light behind him. He was doubled over. When

Marriner walked around the slab he saw that Shanley had the dead arm out from under the sheeting. The forearm rested on his knee. His forehead rested on the forearm. He held her hand in both of his. He was utterly still, and Marriner sensed that the first raw violence of loss had slowly leached out of him here in the acid-smelling silence.

Marriner put his hand on the man's shoulder, squeezed it, shook it gently. "Come on now. I'll take you back."

In a few moments Shanley lifted his head and frowned blankly up at Marriner. "What?"

"I'll take you back to the house now."

Shanley gave a slow nod. He stood up. He lifted the edge of the sheeting and, holding the leaden arm by the wrist, neatly and carefully laid it in at her side and put the sheeting back and gave it a small pat to make it neater.

Marriner walked him out through the dim rooms and out the front door of Gates' place. Six feet beyond the door Shanley stopped abruptly and looked back over his shoulder.

"Why?" he said, his voice loud and hoarsened and despairing.

"Come on along. Mankind has been asking that same damn fool question for two million years, and we'll keep asking it until there's just one last one of us left. And that'll be the last word he says. I'll take you back and give you a little something."

"I don't need it."

"You're getting it anyway."

". . . All right."

On the day she was buried, Shanley drove Jane Weese and old Davie to the church service and then to the cemetery and back to the house. Jane Weese made snorting sobs all the way back. Shanley wished he had been able to weep. There had been the incredulity and the rage, and then the numbness, as if some drug had been injected into his brain. All sights and scents and sounds were vivid but they did not mean very much. It was like living in a very detailed and plausible dream, among people he had imagined.

As he turned into the driveway he saw the stranger on the front steps and hit the brake too hard, startling Jane and Davie.

"Who is that?"

"Why, that's Mr. Fergasson!" Jane said.

He drove to the back of the house, parked there and they got out. He went through the house. Fergasson was in the front hall and made as though to speak, but Shanley went by him and into the study off the living room. The nurse sat knitting.

"No change at all," she said in a voice that seemed too loud for that room. It was a skull covered with wet grey cloth and through some distasteful trick it kept breathing. He despised it for living when all the world's warm flesh was casketed and deep.

When he walked back into the hall Fergasson was there.

"Mr. Shanley, I . . ."

"We'll talk outside."

Fergasson followed him out the front door and around to the wall where, a lifetime ago, Paula had sat in the sun.

"So you're the one who found me."

"I had that good fortune," Fergasson said. He was a tidy little man. He had that servile arrogance of a waiter who feels superior to his customers. "I am sorry about Miss Lettinger. And the old man. And your brother, Mr. Shanley."

"What do you want?"

"Forgive me. This was a strange and tragic mixup. They identified the man. Did you hear? His name was Bertold."

"I heard. What do you want?"

"He was after you, of course. He must have been skilled. But this one went badly for him."

"What do you want?"

"I was curious about you, Mr. Shanley. You have stayed alive a long time. I think you are bright, and lucky."

"Lucky! Oh, yes, I have more luck than I can use."

"You were fond of her."

Shanley frowned at him. And turned and started toward the house. Fergasson called to him. He stopped and turned.

"Mr. Shanley, I just wondered if you were going to keep running."

Shanley stood there a long time. He had the strange feeling that he had remembered something terribly important, something he had been trying to recall for a long time. "Run," he said softly and wonderingly. He moved back toward Fergasson. "No. I don't think I'll run any more."

Fergasson's smile was obsequious. "You'll wait here for them to try again?"

"No."

Still smiling, Fergasson said, "Then what do you think you will do, Mr. Shanley?"

Shanley felt a pain in the corners of his jaw, in the palms of his hands and in the muscles of his back. He felt as if he had come awake. He spoke with an effort. "Wain, Boardman. And other names from them. And other names."

"As soon as the old man dies, Mr. Shanley, you will have ample money. You will have the money, the intelligence, the luck and the hate. It's a rare combination. I have been looking for many years for that combination, Mr. Shanley. It would be a shame to see it all smashed because of—let us say—a combination of rashness and faulty information."

"What do you want of me?"

"I am not a likeable man, Mr. Shanley. But I am a very very clever man, and I am a very thorough man, and I am a very inconspicuous man. I can take a long leave of absence. The firm would not approve of . . . such a hobby. I can add, also, that I am a very indignant man. My indignation has been growing for quite a few years. I can find the names for you, Mr. Shanley. And I can draw maps, make up schedules of daily habits and find appropriate tools of execution. You do not have to like me, Mr. Shanley, in order to use me. And, believe me, without help, you will not live out the month. Unless you run."

Shanley looked at him for a long time. "The running is over."

Just as he took Fergasson's outstretched hand, Shanley

saw the practical nurse coming toward them across the lawn, billowing along through the summer sunlight, wearing such a tight stiff expression of satisfaction that he knew the old man had just died.

THE END
of an Original Gold Medal Novel by
John D. MacDonald

65-10-2